## "We leave at first light."

"*You* leave at first light. I'm not done here." Until she found those kids, she wasn't going anywhere.

He made a sound of disgust. "There's no way I'm letting you stay in this camp without me here to run interference. You'd have been dead, or worse, several times already if I hadn't intervened on your behalf." His voice dropped to a bare thread of sound. "These men are brutal. Violent. No respect for your vocation. I won't let you stay."

"It's not your call," she muttered back.

He must have sensed her stubbornness because he huffed and finally retorted, "I'm bigger than you. I'll throw you over my shoulder and haul you out of here by force if I have to."

"You wouldn't."

His golden eyes glittered in the faint flicker of the fire. "Try me."

D0827993

\* \* \*

Dear Reader,

When I was just getting started writing books, a very wise and famous author told me that the more books I wrote, the harder they would become to write. Alarmed, I asked her why, and she explained that I would find myself digging for deeper and more meaningful themes over the years. She warned me that they would become progressively harder to tackle. And of course, she was exactly right.

In this book, I took on some of my most ambitious themes yet—guilt, redemption, the cost of revenge, the sacrifices we make for family. And, true to that wise author's prediction, this book was particularly difficult to write. But I also learned something in the process. With a little laughter, a pinch of faith and a lot of love, all of us can overcome just about any obstacle life—or writing books—throws into our paths.

My thanks to Ted and Elise for their shining example of how to find love and forgiveness in the midst of chaos. May we all learn a lesson from the two of them and their abiding and steadfast love for one another. I only wish for you, dear reader, as much joyful and fulfilling love in your life, in whatever shape it might take.

It's time now to sit back, kick off your shoes and enjoy Ted and Elise's (entirely fictional) story of how they found one another. Happy reading!

Warmly,

Cindy Dees

# CINDY DEES

## *Soldier's Rescue Mission*

## ROMANTIC
### SUSPENSE

Recycling programs
for this product may
not exist in your area.

ISBN-13: 978-0-373-27759-9

SOLDIER'S RESCUE MISSION

www.Harlequin.com

**Printed in U.S.A.**

**Books by Cindy Dees**

# CINDY DEES

started flying airplanes while sitting in her dad's lap at the age of three and got a pilot's license before she got a driver's license. At age fifteen, she dropped out of high school and left the horse farm in Michigan, where she grew up, to attend the University of Michigan. After earning a degree in Russian and East European Studies, she joined the U.S. Air Force and became the youngest female pilot in its history. She flew supersonic jets, VIP airlift and the C-5 Galaxy, the world's largest airplane. During her military career, she traveled to forty countries on five continents, was detained by the KGB and East German secret police, got shot at, flew in the first Gulf War and amassed a lifetime's worth of war stories.

Her hobbies include medieval reenacting, professional Middle Eastern dancing and Japanese gardening.

This RITA® Award-winning author's first book was published in 2002 and since then she has published more than twenty-five bestselling and award-winning novels. She loves to hear from readers and can be contacted at www.cindydees.com.

This book is, of course, for the real Ted and Elise.
You know who you are!

# Chapter 1

Elise Omayo paused just inside the dim sanctuary of Our Lady of Sacred Hope to soak up the silence and peace of the place. If only she could believe in the things this edifice stood for. She'd give anything to truly embrace ideals like love and faith. Redemption. Now there was a concept. People like her didn't get second chances. Not in this life, and surely not in the next. The best she could hope to do was live out the remainder of her days in a way that didn't add any more to her self-loathing.

"Elise! So good of you to come on such short notice. You look lovely as always." Father Ambrose was a fussy little man, round and soft, but with piercing black eyes that cut through a person's soul like twin lasers. Why he saw anything at all of worth in her, she hadn't the slightest idea.

"You said you have a problem. Of course I came." It was the least she could do for the man who'd talked her down off that bridge five years ago. Literally. Sure, she'd been out of her mind with grief and painkillers and a cocktail of who-knew-what else. But he'd literally climbed up on that railing beside her and convinced her to give him a chance to show her something worth living for. He'd pulled a lost orphan off the streets, given her a home and a purpose, and helped her reach her goal of becoming a nurse. So, here she was. She owed him a favor. A big one.

"Let's go into my office. You look like you could use a nice cup of tea, dear."

Tea? Uh-oh. He must be working himself up to asking her a big favor. Frowning, she followed him.

He hurried down the aisle, pausing briefly to cross himself in front of the altar. Funny how Father A. had never tried to make a Catholic out of her. He said it was God's problem, not his. She wouldn't have made a very good one, anyway, despite her grandmother's best efforts over the years. Too many rituals, too much to remember. Not to mention that whole seven deadly sins business.

She waited patiently while the priest made two cups of steaming hot tea, English-style. When he was finished doctoring it up, the drink tasted more like hot chocolate than tea. She took a sip, promptly burned her tongue, and set the cup down. "Cut to the chase, Father. What do you need? You know I won't say no, so go ahead and blurt it out."

He sighed. "I'm hoping you will do something for me. Something possibly dangerous."

"How dangerous?" She didn't exactly live for thrills and chills, but she'd never shied away from a little risk for a good cause. She'd been known to make house calls in the roughest neighborhoods of New York City in the name of a patient in need.

"I need you to go to Colombia."

*Colombia.* The word rolled over her like a bad dream. Tangled images of jungle and death, poverty and blood, flashed through her mind's eye for an instant before the grief slammed into her. She reeled with the power of it. Just when she thought she'd made her peace with her parents' murders, something went and tore the scab off again like this, leaving a raw and gaping wound in her heart.

Father Ambrose was speaking again. Struggling to breathe, she forced herself to focus on his words. "...pair of children have been orphaned in Colombia and are in need of assistance."

Translation: the kids were caught up in the armed struggle between the Colombian government and one of several paramilitary or drug smuggling organizations currently opposing it. She knew all too well what it was like to be a pawn caught in the middle of that brush war. Belatedly, she choked out, "Who are they?"

"Mia and Emanuel Garza."

She was halfway out of her seat before the names barely crossed the priest's lips. No. No, no, *no.* She saw where this was going. Valdiron Garza had murdered her mother and father. But then the import of the word "orphan" sank in. She sank back down into her seat. "He's dead?" she croaked.

"Yes, my child. He was gunned down in Cartagena a few weeks ago. It is over."

"'It' being her fruitless, and ultimately self-destructive, quest for justice against Garza. Although failing that, she'd have settled for simple revenge.

The priest continued quietly, "I pray you will finally find the peace you seek."

"Who says I seek peace?" she demanded.

"I do."

His simple statement caught her off guard. Forced her

into a moment of sharp self-evaluation. Was he right? *Did* she seek peace? The answer startled her. *Perhaps she did.*

"So Garza's children are stuck in Colombia and looking for a way out. Surely you don't expect me to go save them."

"They are children—"

"Their father tortured and killed my parents!"

"—and innocent—"

"Wait a minute," she interrupted. "How old are these kids?"

"Six and four."

"Oh, my God. They're *babies*. You want me to haul them around in a war zone in the jungle?"

"No. I want you to bring them to me. I will find them decent homes here in America."

"What makes you think I won't just kill them and have my revenge?" she demanded. The sweet taste of it battled on her tongue with the sour knowledge that the Garza children were too young to have participated in their father's atrocities.

Father Ambrose merely gave her a reproachful look. Okay, a reproachful look she deserved. She wasn't a child killer any more than someone who could turn her back on anything small and innocent. Damn him!

He knew she couldn't say no to him. Why this favor? Why not something, anything, else? Something that didn't involve a Garza? Something that didn't involve going back to the killing fields of Colombia? Did he hate her for some reason?

"Look, Padre. I know I owe you my life. And I know I told you to ask me any time, any place, for anything, and if it was in my power to do it for you, I would. But we're talking about Valdiron Garza, here. He was a monster. My parents were peaceful missionaries, and he committed an atrocity against them. How do we know his children won't be the same or worse? Are you sending me to rescue two more future psychopaths? How many people will they kill in their turn? Hundreds? Thousands? More? And besides. What makes you think I could get into and out of Colombia and live?"

"They are very young children. There is plenty of time to mold them into kind, loving adults. And I thought perhaps you should go in dressed as a nun."

"A *nun?*"

"Can you think of a better way to ensure your safety in such a dangerous country? It is a religious place. People will look out for you."

She snorted. "You are much more optimistic than I am that an ugly dress and a wimple will save me."

"And that is why I am Christian and you are not."

"I never said I wasn't Christian."

"You never said you were, either," he retorted gently.

He had her there. In fact, he had her squarely over a barrel. She ought to blow off her promise to help him. Ought to get up and walk out of here right now. She sighed, frustrated. "Where are they?"

"I don't know. But someone who does is reportedly in Santa Lucia. A young man fighting with a rebel group."

"That's down on the border with Bolivia, in the heavy jungle. It's incredibly dangerous territory."

"That is why I called you."

"Expendable, am I?"

"Hardly, Elise. But you are, without question, the most determined person I have ever met. And you know Colombia. If you promise to bring those children to me, you'll move heaven and earth to do exactly that. I have complete faith in you."

"You have a great deal more faith in me than I do," she replied bitterly.

"Just so, my child. Just so."

"But I don't look anything like him!" Ted Fisher stared, aghast, at the photo of the dead man. Even allowing for death's pale patina, Drago Cantori was clearly a fair-skinned European and huge. Although Ted was no slouch in the muscles and fitness department—no special operator was—this Cantori guy looked as if he sucked down steroids like soda. "In case you haven't noticed, boss, I am of African descent. This Cantori guy is…not."

His boss, Navy Commander Brady Hathaway, replied, "We believe Cantori never met his contact in South America. The Army of Freedom insurgents have no idea what he looked like or whether he was black or white. When you show up in place of Cantori they won't know any different."

"You hope," he retorted dryly.

"Captain Fisher, you know more about weapons than anyone else in this facility, not to mention you think well on your feet and speak Spanish like a native. You're the best man for the job."

And that was that. He was going undercover into the jungles of South America on an insanely dangerous op alone and impersonating a dangerous arms dealer. An arms dealer who'd been killed as a side effect of another op to capture Cantori's sister. The mission had been a success and Annika Cantori, a prominent terrorist, was serving life in prison with no possibility of parole. She steadfastly refused to cooperate with the American government, however. Which meant he was on his own.

Drago Cantori had been completely under the U.S. military's radar until he'd surfaced a few months ago. Most of what they knew about his business affairs had been cobbled together from bits and pieces they'd managed to collect from various informants around the world. It was far from a complete picture of the man.

He'd be flying blind for a lot of the mission as he tried to step into the man's shoes and pass himself off as Cantori. Ted picked up the pitifully thin folder that contained everything they knew about the man he was supposed to impersonate. It wouldn't take him ten minutes to memorize everything in here. Talk about going into a mission unprepared. This was a cluster bomb waiting to blow.

Elise tugged at the ill-fitting cardigan sweater bunching up over a dreadful dress. She glanced down at her sensible shoes. They were shockingly comfortable, but she doubted they could've been more hideous looking if someone tried to design them that way. They looked like black bricks on the ends of her legs. In this getup, she hardly needed the black wimple covering her hair to announce that she was a nun. Or at least, doing a darned good impersonation of one.

Now to find the local cantina. That would be where anyone with any influence in Santa Lucia would hang out. It would've been a pretty little town with white, stucco buildings in the Spanish style, were it not for the general poverty and decay enveloping it. But then, the jungle was hard on everything. Car transmissions were torn up by the rutted roads, mildew destroyed textiles, and disease ran rampant in the tropical climate.

It might have been another village three years ago. Different name, different patch of jungle. But the same hopeless desperation clung to the place. This was the Colombia that had cost her both of her parents in a moment of senseless violence.

She hated this place, she hated this place, she *hated* this place. How Father Ambrose had manipulated her into doing this job, she still wasn't quite sure. It had been on the tip of her tongue to tell the priest where he could go, yet here she was. The man was an evil genius, collar or no.

She passed a pair of women even shorter than her, which was saying something. She barely topped five foot two. Aah. There. A faded painting of a foaming beer mug beside a doorway. She ducked into the vestibule and pushed open a heavy, mahogany door.

Every pair of eyes in the joint stared. *That's right. Nun in the house. Be afraid, boys. Very afraid.* She slid into a booth and waited for the barkeep to come over to her resentfully.

"I'll have whatever soda you've got in a can or bottle," she said in polite Spanish.

"You planning to stay long?" the guy growled.

Guilt and beer didn't mix, apparently. In the two days she'd spent in this costume traveling here, the predominant reaction to her wimple from everyone had been reflexive shame. It would've been hilarious if she hadn't been so worried about passing for a nun in this heavily Catholic country. "Am I bad for business?" she asked innocently.

He looked startled. "Yes, actually. You are."

"Then tell me where I can find the Army of Freedom and I'll get out of here."

The barkeep lurched. "What does a woman of the cloth want with people like that?"

"Church business," she replied shortly.

The man frowned, but she didn't elaborate. Valdiron Garza, Chief of Internal Security for the Colombian Army—better known as Chief of Terrorizing Anyone Who Tangled With Garza—had been arguably the most hated man in Colombia. He'd been an equal opportunity murderer, killing people on both sides of the armed conflict between the government and rebel insurgents. News that his children were nearby would spark a feeding frenzy of Garza's victims out for revenge of their own against the kids. As much as she'd hated Garza, she couldn't transfer that hate to a pair of innocent young children. In fact, her main emotion for them was fear for their safety. Not to mention she'd given Father Ambrose her word that she'd keep them safe.

The bartender left to fetch her soda and she risked a glance around the place. It was full of hard men with harder gazes. They didn't like her being here and they weren't afraid to let it show. Wimple or no wimple, it made her nervous. Very nervous. Missionaries got murdered and nuns got assaulted in places like this.

A bottle of grape soda slammed down onto the table before her and she jumped. "What do I owe you?" she asked.

"On the house if you'll take it and leave now."

She sensed a subtle warning in the man's voice. If she stayed any longer, she would get into trouble. Panic leaped in her throat. This place, this whole cursed country, scared her to death. And frankly, she wasn't the type to run around facing down her fears for fun. Every cell in her body screamed at her to get out of here and go home to nice, safe, New York City.

She slid out of the booth, grabbed the warm bottle and stepped out into the muggy afternoon. Today was overcast and relatively cool—only in the mid-eighties. She remembered all too well how this place felt on a hot day with the sun beating down. Saunalike. As it was, she felt as though she was swimming down the street.

Now what was she supposed to do? She had no further

plan for locating the Army of Freedom beyond asking in the cantina. She headed for a little park she'd spotted from the bus on the way into town. As she walked, she sipped at the soda. Yuck. It tasted like cough syrup.

A cement park bench beckoned and, weak-kneed, she sank onto it, overcome by her terror. Squeals of laughter came from a small playground in the park, but even the joy of children couldn't convince her this place was anything other than a hellhole promising death to her.

"Mind if I sit, Sister?"

She jerked sharply. Her gaze snapped up to the tall, dark silhouette belonging to the quiet baritone. "Uh, no."

He sank to the bench beside her but still towered over her. "What brings you to Santa Lucia, ma'am?"

Her heart raced even harder. An urge to run screaming nearly overcame her. She choked out, "Who's asking?"

The man's eyebrows shot up. Whoops. That probably didn't sound nunlike enough. She amended hastily, "I go where the Lord sends me." There. Better.

"Gustavo said you were asking after the Army of Freedom."

Wow. That was fast for word to have gotten to the Army that she was asking about them. She wasn't sure if she was more dismayed or relieved that things hadn't changed at all since the last time she'd been in this godforsaken corner of the world. "Who's Gustavo?"

"Bartender."

"Aah." She waited for the man to continue, but he didn't. It gave her a chance to study his chiseled features. His skin was walnut-stained brown and his short black hair neat and curly, speaking of an African heritage. But his eyes were a contrasting golden hazel that fairly glowed against his dark coloring. And those shoulders! *Aye, caramba.* Muscles bulged in all the right places.

A fine specimen of a man, to be sure—she broke off the train of thought abruptly—she was supposed to be a nun, for crying out loud. Lest he spot the rich appreciation in her eyes, she looked down hastily.

"Well?" he demanded.

"Well what?"

Her companion huffed. "What do you want with the Army?"

Sensing no immediate threat from him, her pulse began to slow. She answered honestly, "I want to find them."

"Why?"

She frowned. "Gustavo no doubt told you it's church business, so why are you pressing me?"

"Because it's not safe for a woman—a person—like you to have any dealings with them."

Amusement quirked her mouth. Apparently, she didn't qualify as an actual woman anymore. "How do you know it's not safe?" she challenged.

"Are you really here alone?"

All questions and no answers, this guy was. "Why do you sound so surprised? It's not like I have anything to fear. I'm a woman of the cloth."

He snorted. "Cloth doesn't provide a hell of a lot of protection from certain threats in this neck of the woods."

*No kidding.* "Are you trying to warn me of something specific?"

"I'm telling you to go back where you came from and leave the Army of Freedom alone."

"I'm sorry. I can't do that. I have business with them."

He scowled but eventually shrugged. "It's your neck." And with that pronouncement, he stood up. As he strode away from her, she took a moment to enjoy his long legs, tight buns, and mile-wide shoulders. A fine specimen of a man, indeed.

Belatedly, it hit her. He had some connection to the Army of Freedom. Why else would he have gone out of his way to ask her what she wanted with that bunch? She waited until he was a block or so away and rose to follow him. He was a full foot taller than her and she had to hurry not to lose him as he strode with those long legs toward the edge of town. Dismayed, she watched him climb into a Jeep and start the engine. *She mustn't lose him.* As sure as she was standing here, he was heading out into the jungle to warn the local Army of Freedom guys that some crazy nun was poking around asking questions about them. The last thing she needed was to spook the contact among that bunch whose family was currently hiding Garza's children.

The Jeep pulled out of its parking spot. She was losing him! Looking around quickly, she spied a moped parked on the sidewalk. *She shouldn't.* But her lead to the Army of Freedom was leaving. She would go to hell for sure if she stole something while wearing a nun's habit. But the alternative was to fail two small children and a priest. It would be acceptable if she just borrowed it, right?

She raced over to the scooter, checking frantically for a key. *Nada.* She popped open the under-seat storage area and spied a flash of metal. Snatching the spare key, she jammed it in the ignition. It wasn't theft if God's work was being done, was it? And besides, theft wasn't one of the seven deadly sins. She would return the moped as soon as she found out where Mr. Tall, Dark and Hunky was going.

The Jeep took a dirt road, which cut into the heavy jungle crowding the margins of the village. The ruts were incredible, some deep enough to nearly swallow her and the moped whole. But the horrible road slowed the vehicle ahead enough that she was able to keep the sound of the engine in range. It took concentration to guide her scooter around the worst of the craters.

The road, such as it was, deteriorated into little more than twin dirt paths. She had to duck hanging vines and was soaking wet from midthigh down with muddy water by the time the Jeep's engine suddenly cut off. Alarmed, she cut her moped's motor and listened hard. Nothing but the screeches and clicks of the jungle echoed around her.

She leaned the motor bike against a tree and proceeded forward cautiously on foot. Those shoes were becoming more sensible by the second as they held up to the rough hike. Her sexy little Louboutins would have been destroyed in a dozen steps.

She spied a lightening in the gloom ahead and slowed down. Were those voices she heard? And what was that growling noise? A portable power generator, maybe? Her heart leaped into her throat. Every cell in her body shouted at her to turn and flee. If she had half a brain, she'd listen to those urges. But no. She'd made a promise. She was going to kill Father Ambrose when she got home. *If* she got home.

Something cold and hard touched the back of her neck, and an audible click made her freeze. She knew that sound. It was a pistol hammer cocking. Oh, God. Her panic turned into head-to-foot trembling.

"You don't take no for an answer, do you, Sister?" A familiar, deep voice rumbled in her ear. Hunky Guy from the park.

"I'm not known for giving up, no," she managed to answer without squeaking too badly.

"Next time you follow someone, steal a moped with a muffler," he muttered. The gun nudged her neck. "Move."

When did his voice start sounding so threatening, anyway? Gulping, she walked forward. Here went nothing.

## Chapter 2

Ted swore under his breath. How on God's green earth had this tiny little nun found her way out here into the middle of nowhere? Obviously, she'd followed him. But why? Didn't she have any sense of self-preservation whatsoever? He was a hard man, used to seeing and doing hard things, but killing a nun was not on his top ten list of favorite recreational activities.

"Were you planning to just stroll into camp and say hello?" he demanded incredulously.

Her slender shoulders shrugged under a nasty, gray-green sweater. "Something like that."

At least with his gun at her back she would make it into the camp alive. Had she just shown up, he had no doubt his comrades would've gunned her down long before they registered the wimple on her head. Unless someone got a good look at her exotic eyes and creamy latte skin and decided to have a little fun first. A wisp of silky mocha hair peeked out by her right ear and he tore his gaze away from the delicate flesh below her earlobe.

"Hola, Enrique!" he shouted. "It's me."

"Drago, my friend. What have you brought us?"

He made eye contact with Enrique, the leader of this particular cell of would-be revolutionaries. What they lacked in organization, they made up for in stubborn will. He could mold them. Use them for his own purposes. His gaze hardened. "I found this lady in the jungle. Apparently, she wants to save our souls."

Stunned silence greeted his announcement as two dozen mercenaries and criminals took in the woman standing before him. A fine trembling passed from his captive to the weapon pressed against the back of her neck. Smart lady. She *should* be afraid of these men. She was perilously close to death. And there might not be anything he could do to stop her from dying.

He frowned. Not that he should care one way or the other if this lunatic wanted to traipse out here and get herself killed. It was her life. He shrugged and nudged her forward.

"Hello, gentlemen," she said in a honey-sweet voice that shouldn't belong to a nun.

"What is this?" Enrique demanded. "A *nun?*" he swore in a distinctly un-Christian fashion.

"I mean you no harm," she intoned. "I come in peace."

Ted snorted behind her. Right. Peace. In the middle of a bunch of paramilitary insurgents armed to the teeth. Or about to be armed to the teeth when he completed his weapons sale to them.

"Drago, introduce us to the good Sister."

"Tell them your name," he ordered her roughly.

"I'm Elise." She corrected hastily, "Sister Mary Elise. And all of you are God's creatures as much as I am."

He thought he caught a note of wry...something...in her voice. Odd.

"Come sit with me, Sister," Enrique invited with patently false courtesy. Ted's hackles rose. Dammit, this woman's safety was not his job! He had bigger fish to fry than a crazy nun in the jungle.

When she didn't budge, he shoved her gently. "Do as he says or he'll gun you down where you stand," he muttered.

She threw him an alarmed look of entreaty over her shoulder. Aw, hell. Did her eyes have to be so big and wide and dark—all soft and helpless and innocent like a puppy? Since when were nuns so damned adorable? Irritated, he took her by the elbow and bodily moved her forward lest Enrique lose his notorious temper right here and now.

He pushed her down into a folding chair in front of a scarred wooden table. "Sister Mary Elise. Welcome to the Army of Freedom. Speak your piece and then get out of here. You can start by explaining what the hell you're doing here."

"I...um...travel to remote corners of this country in search of people who need my ministrations."

Enrique growled, "What is a ministration? We don't need no sermons from no ministers around here."

"I'm a nurse. I deliver babies—" she broke off, glancing at the all-male party that had drawn around her in a menacing circle and which clearly was not in need of her midwifery services "—and, um, give vaccinations. I treat wounds, set sutures and can perform minor surgery in a pinch."

Enrique's shoulders inched down slightly.

"I cook, too."

That got interested looks from everyone. Ted snorted mentally. He'd tasted this bunch's swill, and it was nasty even by his rough standards. He didn't want to know what critters found their way into the gamey and unpleasant stews he'd been forcing down.

"Oh, and I sew. I can mend clothes and do some basic tailoring."

Now she was talking. A woman like her could be distinctly useful in a primitive camp like this.

"Do you offer any other...services?" Enrique asked suggestively.

Ted leaned forward. "Climb up out of the gutter onto the curb, man. She's a nun for goodness' sake. She's offering to do jobs for your men that they could desperately use. That cut on Olivedo's leg is as infected as hell, and all the men have various degrees of jungle rot. And I don't know about you, but I could use a decent meal for a change."

"If you have corn flour, I can make *arepas* for everyone," she offered helpfully, sensing an ally.

*Arepas* were a local fried flatbread, and the mere thought of the fresh, puffy delicacy made his mouth water. He caught swallows and gulps all around him.

Grinning, Ted announced, "There you have it. Keep your paws off her, and she'll make you *arepas* and heal your men. I'd say that's a fair trade."

Enrique, suggestible as always, nodded. Not the brightest bulb in the bin, that guy. But he was a hell of a fighter with fists or a knife, and he commanded his men's fear and respect. "Get to work, woman."

Ted sat back, amused, as she marched over to the sluggish fire like a tiny general and examined the haphazard pile of cooking utensils critically.

"I need a basin of clean water," she announced. "These don't look like they've been washed in months. It's a wonder you're not all dead of food poisoning."

In short order, she was giving commands in that sultry-soft voice of hers, and hardened fighters were racing around gathering the supplies she'd need to make a proper meat filling for the puffy breads in the pan over the fire. It took a good chunk of the afternoon for the feast to come together, but finally, a plate was passed to him and he sunk his teeth into a meat pastry that melted in his mouth. Groans of delight broke out all around him. The nun had just bought herself another day or two of life. She was safe until the next time she crossed Enrique's uncertain temper.

Darkness fell abruptly in the jungle and the night sounds grew loud around the isolated camp. A fire crackled pleasantly and everyone not posted to guard duty lounged around it, savoring a surprisingly tasty local beer that had been broken out as a treat to go with the nun's delicious *arepa* feast.

"Tell me about that deal you did in Africa a few months back, Drago. I hear it changed the course of a war."

Ted's face froze. Crap. What deal? This was exactly what he'd feared would happen when he tried to impersonate the real Drago Cantori.

"Which one?" he asked casually. "Libya?"

The rebel leader frowned. "No. Tunisia."

"Aah. That war," Ted replied, hoping he didn't sound as lame as he felt.

Enrique examined him far too closely for comfort. "You've turned the tide of more than one war, then?"

Ted shrugged. "I merely provide the tools. What men do with them is up to them."

The nun sniffed in displeasure, but he ignored her, concentrating on reading Enrique's body language. It was vital that the guy buy his line of bull.

"How big was the shipment you sent to Tunisia?" Enrique persisted. "How many guns did it take to tip the tide of the uprising into a victory? What kind of weapons did you sell them?"

Nothing in their file on Drago Cantori had indicated that he'd done business in that north-African nation. Ted cast back in his memory for surveillance images he'd seen from that conflict. The freedom fighters had carried mostly outdated, bolt action rifles and basic grenade launchers.

He answered cautiously, "They got mostly surplus weapons from eastern Europe. A few grenade launchers. Ammunition was what they were really desperate for."

"But what about that surface-to-air missile? The one that shot down that Tunisian fighter jet that all the news agencies filmed going down in flames?"

Drago'd sold that thing to the rebels? His colleagues had speculated for months over where that had come from. Some people had believed it was a Tunisian Army missile either shot by accident at a friendly target, or perhaps by a turncoat within the Tunisian army.

"Where'd you get the missile?" Enrique insisted.

"Russia," Ted answered shortly.

Enrique looked confused. "I thought you said it was French."

Damn, damn, damn. This guy had communicated with the real Drago at some point in the past? Ted answered quickly, "The missile was French-made. But I got it in Russia." He didn't like that suspicious look in Enrique's eyes one bit. This guy smelled deception and had enough experience to listen to his instinct.

The nun broke the tension of the moment by announcing, "Well, I can see I'll have my work cut out for me if I start praying for your soul."

He turned to her gratefully, eager to draw everyone's

attention to her and away from his gaffes. "I'm just doing my job, Sister. Someone has to do it, so why not me?"

"You provide weapons that kill people," she stated.

"How is what you do any different?" he demanded.

"I heal the people your guns shoot!"

He shrugged. "Same difference. You patch these men up so they can go back to war and kill some more. You're helping the rebels as much as, or maybe even more than, I am."

The rebels laughed and commenced ribbing the nun about whose soul needed the most praying for, and he let out a careful breath. That had been close. Too close.

As men started drifting away to their tents, Ted noticed to his disgust that Enrique and a few of his top lieutenants were eyeing the pretty nun again. He leaned over to ask her under his breath, "You don't happen to have a tent in that satchel of yours, do you?"

"No. It's all medical supplies."

He swore quietly. In a louder voice, he announced, "The sister will take my hut. I'll sleep outside." *And guard her.*

Enrique's expression fell as he caught Ted's unspoken warning to keep his paws off the nun. Pervert.

He waited for her to return from the latrine pit and held the canvas flap of his half tent, half wooden shack for her. "Don't come out until morning if you value your virtue or your life," he murmured as she passed close to him.

She glanced up at him, her eyes positively doelike. He jolted. A guy could lose himself in eyes like that. *Hello. Nun, here.* The lady was strictly off-limits. Even he wasn't that big a scumbag.

"Thank you for your protection," she murmured back.

So. She wasn't that dumb, after all. She'd realized the mortal danger she was in, and furthermore, she was aware of the delicate dynamic between him and Enrique. He dared not challenge the man's dominance of this cell lest the rebels turn on him, but Enrique needed his weapons and dared not piss him off, either.

He set up a camp cot across the doorway of his make-shift hut and listened to the little noises of the nun settling down for the night. Something about the sounds women made was just sexy. It was easy to envision her peeling off those frumpy clothes and rinsing the mud off her legs with the washcloth and pitcher of water he'd put inside for her.

She'd be brushing out her hair now. How long was it, anyway? Did nuns shave their heads or something under those wimples? Except he'd seen a lock of it peeking out earlier. It had been dark and smooth and touchable. The whole woman was so damned touchable. And yet, she was totally off-limits. Such an odd little nun.

He'd done his damnedest through the day not to let his thoughts go there, but as he sank toward sleep, his formidable mental control slipped. It was no stretch to imagine what she looked like under that god-awful dress. Her waist had been tiny, her shoulders slender, the bones delicate. She'd be a looker, all right, all feminine curves and soft seduction.

He jolted back to full alertness. *Stop. It.* She was a nun. Hands off. End of discussion. No matter how long it had been since he'd seen or had another woman, he was not even going to contemplate any shenanigans with Sister Mary Elise.

The gentle rise and fall of her breathing came from the other side of the thin canvas wall long before he finally followed her into unconsciousness.

A scream tore Elise from a surprisingly deep sleep sometime in the wee hours of the night. Her nose was cold, and Drago's blankets were pulled practically over her head. Groans and more screaming were forthcoming.

She'd worked the trauma unit in a New York City hospital long enough to know someone was badly injured out there. She went into action automatically. She grabbed her sweater and threw it on, and glancing around, grabbed a pair of sweat pants wadded up in the corner. She dragged them on, jammed her feet into the black bricks without tying them, snatched up her medical bag, and stumbled outside.

"Where is he?" she demanded without preamble.

Drago was kneeling on the ground, shirtless and entirely glorious. He pointed across the clearing. "I'll be there in a sec."

She raced to the fire, where a man thrashed on the ground in the midst of several other men. "Step aside," she ordered in her no-nonsense, E.R. nurse voice. The insurgents leaped out of the way.

"What happened?" she asked tersely as she dropped to her knees beside the mound of blood and torn flesh that had once been a man's gut.

"Jaguar attack," someone offered up.

The jagged tears in parallel lines across the man's midriff seemed to confirm that. She yanked out scissors and began cutting away the remnants of the guy's shirt. At least his innards were still mostly in place. The peritoneum was compromised, though. Without massive antibiotics, and soon, the man was a goner. But first things first. She had to stop the bleeding and sew him back together enough to make it to a hospital and good drugs.

"I need someone to hold this pad here." Strong brown hands materialized in her line of sight. She glanced up to see Drago's grim face. She nodded, and he took over applying pressure to the worst of the other wounds as she started sewing on the patient.

Thankfully, the victim passed out quickly. Whether from blood loss or shock or overwhelming pain, she didn't know. But at least he'd stopped that screaming. She'd learned in her job to block it out, but it was nice not to have to.

When the life-threatening bleeding had been stopped, the tedious business of quilting the guy's gut back together commenced. Shockingly, Drago picked up a suture needle and pitched in, doing a darned credible job of setting sutures on his side of the guy's belly. She'd lay odds the guy had some sort of formal medical training.

Eventually, she sat back on her haunches. "Done. I've given him all the penicillin I've got, and that should hold him through the night. But in the morning, he needs to get to a hospital and have a whole lot more antibiotics if he's going to have any chance of pulling through."

Enrique nodded, not looking particularly concerned. Death was apparently a common and fairly casual affair for these men.

"I'll drive him to town in the morning," Drago announced quietly.

She glanced over at her impromptu assistant. "Thank you."

He shrugged and offered a hand down to her. She straightened painfully, her legs cramped from two hours of kneeling on the cold ground.

As they walked back toward the ramshackle structure that passed for his quarters, he commented, "There's nothing more you can do for him tonight. Let's catch a little sleep before we go."

She stopped. "You can go back to town. But I'm staying here."

"No. You're not."

The words were uttered quietly, but with unmistakable authority. Obviously, this was a man used to having his orders followed. Tough. She didn't work for him, and she had a job of her own to do out here. She had yet to make contact with the insurgent whose family was hiding the Garza children. And until she found those kids, she wasn't going anywhere.

She commenced walking again. "I'm not going to argue with you—"

"Good. We leave at first light."

"*You* leave at first light. I'm not done here."

He made a sound of disgust. "You have no idea how done you are here."

She paused in the doorway of his shack. "I'm not kidding—"

He interrupted her yet again. "Neither am I. There's no way I'm letting you stay in this camp without me here to run interference. You'd have been dead, or worse, several times already if I hadn't intervened on your behalf." His voice dropped to a bare thread of sound. "These men are brutal. Violent. No respect for your vocation. I won't let you stay."

"It's not your call," she muttered back.

He must have sensed her stubbornness because he huffed and finally retorted, "I'm bigger than you. I'll throw you over my shoulder and haul you out of here by main force if I have to."

"You wouldn't."

His golden eyes glittered in the faint flicker of the fire. "Try me."

There were any number of things she'd like to try with him, but being hauled out of here over his shoulder was *not* one of them. Clearly, there was no reasoning with the man.

And standing here arguing with him wasn't doing any good. She'd explain things to him in the morning when they'd all had some rest.

But how she was going to convince him she had to stay with this bunch of murderous cutthroats without mentioning the Garza children, she had no idea. She'd cross that bridge tomorrow. Right now her eyes were burning, her shoulders ached and she was cold. She just wanted to crawl into the bed that smelled deliciously like this man's aftershave and crash.

A light touch, stroking through her hair, woke Elise gradually. The night sounds of the jungle had given way to a chorus of chirping and squawking, birds mostly. It must be morning. Although she couldn't tell with her face completely buried under the blankets. She inhaled the intoxicating scent of the man who normally slept in this bed and sleepily imagined him draped over her like a warm blanket.

The fingers stroked her hair again, slowly. With sensual appreciation. She started to turn into the caress before she woke enough to remember. *Nun.* Cursing under her breath, she threw the covers off her head and rolled over to protest the intimate wake-up call.

Drago towered over her, a perplexed frown on his handsome features.

"Did my patient make it through the night?" she asked.

"Yes. But he's feverish. Sweating. Swelling and abdominal pain."

"Peritonitis," she announced. "I was afraid of that."

Drago shrugged. "It was inevitable."

"He's going to need massive infusions of antibiotics," she replied. She left unsaid the part where, even then, the man's survival was going to be a dicey thing.

"The sooner the better," the arms dealer replied. "Regardless of your objections last night, I'm going to need you to ride to town with me to watch your patient. He's getting delirious and we can't have him tossing around and tearing his stitches. Then he'd die for sure."

She scowled and sat up, clutching the blankets to her chest. She wore only a camisole under the covers and, nun or no nun, wasn't about to flash him a bunch of skin way out here in the jungle by herself. Darn him, he'd struck upon the one argument she couldn't refute. If the injured man needed her nursing skills, she couldn't very well deny him her aid.

"You're taking advantage of my duty as a nurse," she grumbled.

He held out her dress and turned away so she could throw back the covers and shiver into it. "Of course I am. I play to win, Sister."

She glared at his back. Jerk. She yanked on her sweater, thankful for its meager warmth and uncaring of its bread-mold color this morning. By the time she got back from the latrine pit, Drago was supervising the loading of the unconscious man into the back of his Jeep.

Elise eyed the moped, which had been brought into the camp overnight, with regret. "I really need to return that to its owner."

Drago rolled his eyes and muttered rapidly to one of the revolutionaries. "It's taken care of. Now get in the car. We're leaving."

Her gaze narrowed. She never had dealt well with high-handed men. "Don't give me orders, buster."

Enrique cackled from the other side of the injured man's stretcher. "Oh! The little nun has claws! Be careful Drago, or you'll get torn up like Robson here."

She knew better than to rise to the revolutionary's bait

and merely climbed in the back of the Jeep beside her patient in grim silence. It annoyed the hell out of her to have gotten so close to her goal, only to have to retreat now. But she'd be back, by golly. Those children, and Father Ambrose, were counting on her.

# Chapter 3

Ted glanced in the rearview mirror yet again and grinned at the thunderous scowl on the nun's face. Didn't like being manipulated against her will, did she? Feisty little thing. "How's he doing?" he asked.

"In shock. But at least he's not flailing around."

"Think he'll make it?"

She shrugged like a seasoned medical professional. "I give him about even odds. It'll depend on how strong and healthy he was before and how well his system fights the infection."

"The locals are tough. Surviving this jungle is not for the weak." And speaking of which, now that he had her by herself, he demanded, "What were you really doing out there? Why did you want to march into that camp? There was no way you were getting out alive without me. Do you have a death wish?"

"Do you always ask so many questions?" she replied blandly.

Irritation flared in his gut. "Answer me."

Her dark gaze met his in the rearview mirror. She stared at him for a long time as if measuring him. She stared for so long he actually began to worry that she might be seeing more than he wanted her to. She was a nun, after all. And people of the cloth were in the business of knowing human nature. Did she see through the ruse? Horror washed over him. She mustn't blow his cover! He broke the eye contact and focused on the dirt road before him.

"Who are you?" she asked.

He swore under his breath. She knew he wasn't what he appeared to be, dammit.

"My name's Drago. Drago Cantori."

"Where are you from, Drago Cantori? Why were you hanging out with the Army of Freedom? You're not Colombian."

"I'm French. Or more precisely, Basque." Please God, let her not speak the Basque tongue. It was a thankfully rare language, but he'd been completely hopeless at mastering anything beyond a few of the most basic phrases of it in the few days he'd had to prepare for this mission.

"Hmm. I had you pegged for an American."

He jolted and grasped the steering wheel more tightly to hide his shock. "Why's that?" he asked cautiously.

"Your accent. There are shades of American vowels in your Spanish."

She must have a hell of a good ear. He usually had no trouble passing for a native South American. Enrique had pegged him for a Peruvian. Of course, the insurgent hadn't looked too far past the duffel bag full of weapons he and his men would give their right nuts to have.

"I spent some time in the States," he explained cautiously. And please God, let her not ask for details.

Thankfully, she pressed him in another direction. "What were you doing with Enrique and his men? You're not seriously planning to give them grenade launchers and missiles, are you?"

Thank goodness. Safe ground. "Not that it's any of your business, but I was about to close a deal to sell them a supply of basic firearms and ammunition when Einstein, here, went and got himself hurt. Instead, I'm an ambulance driver now."

"Ingratiating yourself to Enrique, are you? Was he reluctant to do the deal?"

He swore mentally. This woman was entirely too perceptive for her own good. "Not at all. He's eager to introduce me to his superiors so I can do an even bigger deal for the entire Army of Freedom."

She tsked. "And here you are, having to rescue the nun and the hurt guy, instead. It must gall you to have to play Boy Scout."

"You could cost me a great deal of money if I lose this sale," he allowed.

"I'd apologize, but I can't say as I'm sorry that hundreds of people won't be gunned down by your weapons."

He sighed. "If the Army of Freedom doesn't get the guns from me, they'll get them from someone else."

"You're actually pulling out the 'it's not the gun, it's the person using it' argument?"

He scowled. "Yes, I am. The gun isn't the thing. It's merely a tool. The person pulling the trigger makes the decision to commit violence."

"Without the tool, he couldn't make the decision at all," she shot back.

"If a person's determined enough, they'll use their fists. Or a rock. Or a stick."

"Aah, but a gun is ever so much more efficient, isn't it?"

He shook his head. "How about we agree to disagree on this one, Sister?"

She fell silent and busied herself checking on her patient. But twin spots of red stained her cheeks. Didn't like letting go of the argument, apparently. Must be a flaming idealist at heart. Which was no surprise, given her profession. But he was a pragmatist. He'd love for the world to be chock-full of peace-loving souls like her. However, until that day came, the world would continue to need people like him to protect people like her.

The dirt road had dried out a little overnight, and the trip back to Santa Lucia went relatively quickly, if still tooth-jarringly bumpy. He pulled up in front of the one-story building that was more regional clinic than hospital and jumped out of the Jeep. He fetched the doctor and lone nurse from inside, and with Elise's help, the four of them horsed the wounded man to a bed inside. In short order, an IV drip was set up and antibiotics started pumping into the man's arm.

Elise—why did he have so much trouble thinking of her as Sister Elise?—fussed over her patient until she was satisfied the doctor would take adequate care of the guy. Ted leaned against a wall, arms crossed, and waited her out. Finally, she fell silent.

"You done telling the doctor how to do his job?" he asked in English.

She scowled and made a distinctly un-nunlike face at him. "Let me just replenish my supply of penicillin and suture thread, and then you can take me back to camp."

Over his dead body.

He waited until she was seated beside him in the Jeep to spell out the score to her. "Okay. Once and for all, you're not going back to that Army of Freedom camp. You will die. I will take you anywhere else you want to go—" he amended quickly, given who he was talking to "—I'll take you anywhere else *safe* you want to go. But I can't in good conscience let a nun die."

"Oh, so you have a conscience now?" she snapped.

*Not* a line of questioning he was eager to pursue. Instead, he pressed the automatic door locks to emphasize the fact that she was at his mercy and asked implacably, "Where can I take you?"

Surprisingly, she didn't blow her stack. Instead, she studied him intently, the way she had before, as if she was taking his measure as a man. He cringed to think about what she would see in him. Did the violence that had been part of his life for so long show on his face?

"Who are you, really?" she asked quietly.

Cripes! What did she see when she looked at him? "We're not talking about me. We're talking about you, Sister. Where can I take you? You're not getting out of this vehicle until I've deposited you somewhere reasonably safe for a nun."

"Is anywhere in this godforsaken country truly safe?" she asked with enough bitterness to send his eyebrows sailing upward.

"Probably not. But you know what I mean."

She fell silent and he waited her out. In his experience, very few women could stand silence for long. But as the tension stretched out between them, apparently this woman was the exception to the rule.

He was ready to squirm himself by the time she finally said cautiously, "Can I trust you with a secret?"

Something about her wimple compelled him to answer her truthfully. "Depends on the secret, I suppose."

A frown creased her forehead. "You're not making this easy."

He wasn't known for being an easy man. Never had been. Never would be. He half turned in his seat to face her more fully. "What's going on, Elise?"

The use of her first name minus the title seemed to shock her into stillness. But then she nodded slowly to herself as if she'd arrived at a decision.

"I'm in Colombia to rescue two children who've been orphaned recently. I have reason to believe the family who is hiding them has a member in that Army of Freedom encampment you so effectively yanked me out of this morning. I've got to go back there. Find the contact. Discover where the children are."

"No."

She stomped her foot on the floor in utter frustration. "Don't you understand? I promised. Whether you like it or not, I'm doing this. You can drive me all the way to Texas if you like, but I'll turn around and come right back here."

"No. You will not. You will die, and those children won't get rescued at all."

"You're so infuriating!" she exclaimed.

Talk about the pot calling the kettle black. But her revelation did complicate matters. She wasn't going to be as easy to chase away as he'd thought. He spared a glance over at the stubborn set of her chin and truculent glint in her eyes. Make that impossible to chase away.

"I don't see why you're interfering with this," she persisted. "It's men exactly like you who make most of the orphans in this country parentless."

No, it wasn't. He was one of the good guys, dammit. He stopped the people she was talking about. But it wasn't as if he could tell her that without blowing his cover.

She wasn't his problem. And another pair of orphaned

kids in this war-torn land weren't his problem, either. But that didn't stop his gut from twisting unpleasantly at the way she was looking at him—as though he'd already betrayed her trust.

He had a job of his own to do. He had to stay focused on that. He had to make sure Enrique passed him up the chain of command to the top brass in the Army of Freedom. And that meant he had to go back to Enrique's camp. But there was no way in hell—or heaven—that he was letting this nun go with him.

"What if I find the contact for you?" he asked heavily. "Would you stay here and wait for me?"

"Why would you help me?"

He shrugged. Yet another line of questioning he'd rather not pursue. "Yes or no?"

"Should I trust you?" she asked reflectively.

He couldn't tell if she expected him to answer the question or not, so he chose to ignore it. Besides, he had no idea how to answer it.

"All right. Fine. I'll give you a day before I come back out there."

"A week."

"No way!" she exclaimed. "Two days."

"Four."

"Three."

He nodded briskly. "Deal."

She scowled suspiciously. Smart woman not to trust him.

"Have you got a room in town?" he asked.

"No, I'd just arrived when I met you in that park."

"What possessed you to follow me, anyway?" He started the Jeep and pointed it at the only half-decent hotel in town.

"You knew more about the Army of Freedom than you were telling me."

"And you knew that how?"

She shrugged. "I just knew. You're easy to read."

*Holy Mother of God*— He checked the thought sharply. Probably not an appropriate phrase in the current company.

In short order he rented a room for her in Santa Lucia's lone hotel and installed her in the sparse, if neat, little room. Suddenly, he was frantic to get far, far away from her all-too-perceptive eyes.

"Don't leave here until I get back, or else," he ordered her, more than half-convinced she would disobey him and end up in some new and terrible pickle before he got back to town.

"Or else what?"

Was that a note of playful flirtation in her voice? His gaze snapped to hers, but her eyes were wide and innocent. What was *wrong* with him? She was a *nun!*

Scowling, he retorted, "Or else I'll tell the law you stole that moped, and you'll be thrown in jail." Not to mention, he would seriously consider strangling her when he caught up with her.

"You wouldn't." She sounded genuinely horrified.

"I would." He stalked over to the door and tossed out one last warning and order. "Stay put until I get back. Got it?"

A long-suffering sigh. "Got it."

Why couldn't he stay mad at her? He relented enough to mumble, "I'll be back as soon as I can. I promise."

Elise slept badly that night, tossing and turning in the narrow bed without Drago's scent to comfort her. How could that man make her so crazy and make her feel so safe at the same time? He was an arms dealer, which meant he was anything but safe. And yet, something about him called to her. If only she weren't masquerading as a nun! Of course, she wouldn't have made it this far without the disguise, but still. The restraints of it chafed. Who'd have guessed she'd bump into a smoking-hot guy out here in the wilds of the Colombian jungle?

The next day passed slowly. But the third day was maddening. She was bored to tears, sick of staring at her little room's walls, and she couldn't very well explain to the proprietor that she needed more than the Bible on her bed stand to distract her or she was going to lose her mind soon.

Drago said three days. Had something happened to him? Was he in trouble? Hurt? Captive? In need of rescue? Should she go after him? She was reasonably confident she could find the Army of Freedom camp again. Assuming Enrique hadn't moved it. And what of her contact within that bunch? Would he have given up on someone coming for the children by now? Told his family to just kill the Garza kids and be done with it?

The sun started to set and red light flooded her room, turning the far wall into a sheet of blood. That was when she gave in to the panic, complete with hyperventilation, inability to form coherent thoughts and an overwhelming need to flee for her life. She was a nurse, for goodness' sake. She saw blood all the time and it never freaked her out. But she hadn't been back to Colombia since she lost her folks. And everything about this trip reminded her way too much of the last time she'd been here and seen a wall covered in blood.

Coming here had been a terrible idea. What on earth Father Ambrose had been thinking to trick her into coming down here, she hadn't the slightest idea. Images of her parents flashed through her brain almost too quickly to process. Happy ones of them traveling the Colombian countryside together. Her father praying by lantern light. Her mother's quiet strength as she worked side by side with local women, easing their lives for a few moments. And other images. Bloody. Violent. Sickening.

She slid down the wall, curling up in a ball on the hard, wooden floor. God, she missed them so much. If only she hadn't been so damned young and impatient to strike out on her own and get away from them. If only she'd enjoyed them more while she'd had them, told them more often how much she loved them…

The tears, when they finally came, were hot and painful and plentiful. She cried as though she hadn't cried in years. It was being back in this country that triggered it all. She couldn't do this. It hurt too much. First thing in the morning, she was obtaining a vehicle and getting out of here.

Finally, no more tears came. Wrung out, she climbed into bed numbly. Three days had passed and Drago hadn't come back for her. What had she been thinking to trust the word of an illegal arms dealer? She'd already lost too much time to him. Enough was enough. She was going home.

Sharp regret that he hadn't kept his word disturbed her restless sleep, and maybe that was why she heard her doorknob turning stealthily sometime after midnight. How had the person on the other side of that panel gotten the thing unlocked anyway? She looked around for a weapon, and only the lamp was close at hand. She grabbed it high up by the bulb and flipped it upside down, making an impromptu club of the heavy base. Creeping quietly, she made her way over to the door. Poised to wallop whoever came through it, she held her breath and watched the knob turn by slow degrees.

The door cracked open and a narrow strip of light fell across the floorboards. With a wordless shout, she jumped forward to brain whoever was about to come in.

"Whoa there, Elise!" Drago threw up his arms and blocked his face as she swung the lamp with all her might.

She tried to stop the blow, but the lamp was heavy and she was scared. It landed with a heavy thud on his fore-arm and upper skull. He dropped like a rock to the floor.

Oh, God. Had she killed him? Panicked, she dropped to her knees beside him, checking for bleeding. Did he have a fractured skull or worse? A goose egg was already rising under his short, curly hair. Frantic, she pried one of his eyelids open to check his pupil.

Strong arms whipped up around her, jerking her down to his chest forcefully. Muscle surrounded her on all sides. Delicious, bulging, firm muscle. That smelled good. Lord, he made her feel small and weak and vulnerable. And oh so tempted to do something no nun would even consider.

"If you *ever*—" the words ground out furiously from between his gritted teeth "—hit me like that again—" a second eye opened to glare at her along with the first one "—I swear—" his arms tightened around her until she could barely breathe "—I'll turn you over my knee and spank you until you can't sit down."

She gasped as fury rolled off of him, drowning her in the sheer maleness of it.

"Understood?" he bit out.

"Yes, sir," she replied in a small, chastened voice. "I didn't see who you were until it was too late to stop my swing. Are you okay?"

"My arm hurts. And my head's killing me. Were you some sort of baseball player in your prior life?"

She grinned down at him, and it dawned on her that their mouths were about twelve inches apart. Almost in kissing range. And he had such a kissable mouth. Firm and generous. He seemed like the kind of man who'd take his time and be thorough about it. Warmth made her whole body go soft, and she melted against him…which made his muscular frame feel just that much more wonderful against her body. His heat and hardness were the perfect contrast to her softness.

Their gazes met in the dim light from the hallway and electricity erupted between them. Sex and sparks and sizzling heat all rolled into one incendiary look. Oh, yeah. He was as aware of her as she was of him. And he wanted her the same way she wanted him. And…nothing, darn it! She watched in dismay as horror unfolded in his eyes along with the belated recollection that She. Was. A. Nun.

His arms loosened abruptly. "God, I'm so sorry. I mean, gosh, I'm sorry. I mean…I forgot…please don't be afraid… won't hurt you…respect the church…"

He was babbling at her. Big, bad, tough, arms dealer Drago. It was kind of cute, actually. But it was also so immensely frustrating not to be able to just lean down and kiss the big lug that she could scream! Reluctantly, she squirmed, and his arms fell away from her.

Bracing her hands on his mile-wide chest, she pushed herself up and off of him. But not before the heat of him scorched her palms. *Must resist the delicious man.* More to the point, she *really* must resist the man engaged in the criminal and dangerous activities, regardless of how hot he might be. But good grief, pushing away from him was hard.

Abruptly, his eyes glowed like hot golden embers. She glanced down with a frown and realized she was wearing only a soft cotton camisole and her skimpy bikini panties—the pink satin ones with red hearts and a sassy little bow. Emphatically not the white cotton granny panties Father Ambrose had given her to wear with her nun outfit. But nobody was ever going to see her in her underwear as a nun, right?

Swearing under her breath, she glared at Drago as his gaze slid higher, pausing on the unmistakable swell of her breasts before finally, belatedly, lifting to her face.

She snapped, "Could you have the decency to look away while I get some clothes on?" Her irritation owed a lot more to her reaction to him than his to her. The way those golden eyes had devoured her had made her feel feminine. Sexy. Fabulous.

If she had to keep her hands off the gorgeous arms dealer for very much longer, Father Ambrose was *so* going to owe her for her Herculean restraint. She supposed nuns everywhere would expect her to behave in a manner fitting of their vows. But good grief, it was hard! Especially with Drago sprawled out on her floor like some sort of reclining god.

She glanced over her shoulder at him, and he was obediently staring at the wall to his left. Who'd have guessed an illegal arms dealer could behave with any chivalry at all. For surely, what he was doing wasn't legal. The Colombian government wouldn't be thrilled at the idea of militant insurgents getting their hands on weapons and ammunition.

She yanked the dress over her head—she really was starting to loathe the sack-shaped thing. She silently vowed to cut it into pieces and use it to clean something really nasty when she got home. Or maybe she'd just ritually burn it.

"Can I look now?" Drago rumbled, laughter in his voice.

"I'm decent."

"Honey, you're a whole lot more than—" He broke off while she gaped.

She was a whole lot more than what? And he'd called her honey. Not to mention his voice had been dripping with seduction when he started to make that comment. Was he truly attracted to her? Even in this revolting getup?

"Here. Let me put my wimple on," she said dryly. "Maybe that will help you remember who I am."

He sat up, propping one arm on an upraised knee while he shoved the other hand through his short hair. "I'm sorry…again. I can't seem to get it through my head that you're a nun. You just don't…" He trailed off, looking flummoxed.

She just didn't *what?* She didn't know who was more frustrated, him or her. She would give her right arm to hear how he'd have finished that sentence. But it wasn't as if the nun could go fishing for a compliment, darn it.

She sighed and changed the subject. "Did you have any luck finding the guy who knows about the children?"

"You doubt my skills?" he asked darkly.

It was her turn to be flustered. "I—no—of course not—" She huffed. "So what did you find out?"

"Aren't you going to ask me how my business deal went?"

Okay, that was a definite teasing tone in his voice now. He'd been messing with her a minute ago. Jerk. "No, I'm not asking," she declared. "I think it's reprehensible that you're arming violent and lawless men like Enrique and turning them loose on the population of this country. Hasn't Colombia had enough violence? It's men like you who make the insurgency drag on and on and continue to put children at risk."

He threw up his hands in surrender. "All right, all

right, Sister. I confess: I'm a bad man. Will you forgive my sins?"

"Only a priest can grant you absolution," she snapped. She had no idea if that was true or not, but Drago didn't seem to know any different.

He muttered low enough that he probably hadn't meant for her to hear, "I'd love to do a little penance with you."

She pursed her lips. "Am I going to have to clobber you with this lamp again to knock a little sense into your head?"

Laughing, he scrambled back toward the door. "Please, no. My skull's thick but not that thick. I think you already split my head in two."

"Oh, come now. I can hit a lot harder than that."

His eyes sparkled with humor, glinting like nuggets of pure gold, and her breath caught. With his features relaxed and open like this, it was impossible to believe he was a hardened criminal. "I'll pass on the batting practice," he chuckled.

"Do you need a couple of aspirin? I've got some in my bag."

"No. I'll be fine. I've taken a lot worse hits than that in my day."

"Do tell."

He rose to his feet and, in the tiny room, she was abruptly aware of just how large he really was. Not only did he tower a foot taller than her, but he had to be double her weight. And every ounce of it was rock-solid muscle.

He reached for the hem of his shirt and tugged it up, alarming her mightily until he commented, "Worst hit I ever took was this one." He pointed at a long scar that bisected his torso. "I got it in a knife fight in Rio de Janeiro a few years back."

She examined the scar with a professional eye. "You almost died from that one, didn't you?"

Surprised lit his features. "Yes, I did."

"Heavy blood loss? Punctured lung?"

"Exactly."

"What was the fight about?"

He jolted at her question. She couldn't tell if he was surprised by the topic or just reluctant to tell her. But then he answered glibly, "What else? A woman."

The explanation didn't ring true. But then, why would he lie to her about something like that? She probably ought to say something disapproving about loose morals leading to unpleasant consequences, but she was too riveted by the rippling slabs of abdominal muscle before her to form the sentence.

She spied the edge of another scar, its round pucker distinctive. "When did you get shot?" she asked.

He shrugged. "Hazard of the job."

Hmm. That was not an answer. But it was a beautifully smooth sidestep. "Have you got more than one of those?"

"You want me to take off my shirt so you can count?"

Her gaze jerked to his just as his jerked to hers. Their gazes met in a moment of stunned—and mutual—awareness. Naked attraction shone in his eyes, and there was no way anything else shone in hers. He started to take a step forward and then lurched hard, screeching to a halt. His hands fell to his sides in fists.

"I am *so* sorry. Again. I don't know what's wrong with me." He swore under his breath, a string of epithets completely unfit for the ears of a nun.

She released the shaky breath she'd only just realized she was holding. "Look. I'm not dead. And I am female. There's nothing wrong with you for being aware of either. We just can't do anything about it."

"Agreed."

He closed his eyes for a long moment, and when he opened them, calm pervaded his gaze. She wished she had that much self-discipline. Her admiration for him climbed a notch.

Drago said roughly, "I think I found your guy. Named Juan Ferrosa. He got drunk and was bragging that his sister worked in some rich guy's home. Single father with a couple cute kids. He said the guy got murdered a few weeks back. I'd lay odds his sister pulled the kids out and has hidden them somewhere."

"That's not very helpful," Elise commented. How on earth was she supposed to find a woman and two kids somewhere in Colombia?

"I found out where his sister lives. His mother lives in the same village. I bet sis took the kids home to mama."

She frowned. It was better than nothing. Worth a try, at any rate. "What village?"

"Dinky place called Acuna."

Her parents had been through there a time or two! She replied eagerly, "Acuna's not more than a day's travel upriver from here." The mighty Putumayo River flowed down out of the Andes Mountains in northwestern Colombia and formed much of the country's southern border. The broad body of water was infested with crocodiles, anacondas and even more dangerous humans of various stripes. Natives called it the Icá. Either way, it was a deadly place. And Acuna was in the heart of cocaine country.

"You're not going there alone," Drago announced.

Right. Like she planned to expose small children to an arms dealer and his brand of danger. She rolled her eyes at him. "We've already had this conversation. I'm getting those children and I don't need your help. And I did okay in the Army of Freedom camp. They didn't kill me on sight."

"Because my pistol was already at the back of your head. And I did my damnedest to get them to accept you. For which you have yet to thank me, Sister."

"Thank you," she snapped. And then sighed. "God bless you."

He made a pained face, whether because he wasn't used to doing acts of kindness or because he wasn't used to receiving blessings for them, she couldn't tell.

Silence stretched out between them and threatened to become awkward. To break it, she asked, "How did your business go? Did you get your introduction to the Army of Freedom's leadership?"

"Actually, I did. Turns out they're headquartered in cocaine country. Not all that far from Acuna."

She saw where this was going. In a desperate effort to distract him, she murmured, "Lovely. Now you can sell enough weapons to kill thousands of innocent Colombians instead of just a few hundred. Think of all the orphans you'll create."

He opened his mouth and looked as though he wanted to defend himself, but snapped it closed instead. Strange man. An arms dealer who got defensive about the morality of what he did? Go figure.

"You do know there's no way you're changing my mind about you going to Acuna by yourself, right?" he asked grimly.

"Excuse me?"

He just gave her a "you heard me" look.

To argue or not to argue with him? To date, she'd had no luck whatsoever in budging him once he made up his mind. Direct confrontation clearly wasn't the way to handle this man. It wasn't that she had any intention of caving in to his unreasonable demands. She just had to find another way to go around him.

In any other context, she'd have resorted to batting her eyes and using her feminine wiles on him to get her way. But as a nun, she had only logic and calm reason at her disposal. And with his jaw jutting out like that, he looked totally immune to either logic or reason.

Finally, she said quietly, "If you want to come along, I suppose I can't stop you. But I am going to find those children and take them to safety no matter what."

"Stubborn female," he grumbled. But she thought maybe she caught a hint of grudging admiration in his voice.

"I prefer to think of myself as determined. Goal oriented, if you will."

"Stubborn."

She snorted. "Isn't that a case of the pot calling the kettle black?"

"Absolutely." And unaccountably, he grinned. "You're cute when you get all indignant."

He thought she was cute? Cool.

"When do you want to leave?"

She looked up at him, startled.

"How about first light?" he suggested in answer to his own question. "I could use a little shut-eye. Haven't had much rest the past few days."

Now that he mentioned it, there were dark shadows around his eyes that hadn't been there before, and a certain hollow exhaustion clung to him. The nurse within her kicked into gear. "When's the last time you slept?"

He shrugged. "I can go on stim pills for five days if I have to."

"You haven't slept since you left town three days ago, have you?" she accused.

His gaze slid away from hers. Uh-huh. She was right. Her inner nurse kicked in hard. "You lay your heinie down on that bed right now and close your eyes, mister. Stimulant pills may work for a while, but the crash afterward is murder."

"But it's your bed—"

She cut him off. "Horizontal. Now."

"Yes, ma'am." A grin flickered on his mouth as he stretched out on the narrow bed.

She pulled the covers up over him, but they only came to his chest. She tucked them in around him, nonetheless, clucking like a mother hen all the while. "Three days without sleep? What were you thinking? Don't you know how hard that is on your body? You need rest, Drago. Close your eyes. Go on. Sleep."

He closed his eyes, but a grin spread across his face at her fussing. She jammed the covers under his shoulder more tightly. "And quit grinning like the cat who swallowed the canary."

"Mmm. Tasty canary," he murmured, already sounding half-unconscious.

She tiptoed to the doorway and slipped out into the hall, pulling the door shut behind her. There was a nice sofa in the lobby she could stretch out on and catch a nap. Goodness knew, she'd slept on worse. Once, during a triple shift in the E.R. she'd lain down on a stainless-steel cadaver slab for a nap. She'd been so cold when she woke up she could hardly move.

Tugging her sweater around her, she tucked her toes between the sofa cushions and fell asleep with thoughts of Drago in her mind and a smile on her face.

## Chapter 4

Ted woke up slowly. He was comfortable. Relaxed. Well-rested. And all three sensations were terribly *wrong*. Frowning, he opened his eyes. Sunlight crept past the edges of the faded curtains. And his feet were cold. He bent his knees, pulling them up under the bottom edge of the blanket tucked under his chin but not quite reaching the bottom of the bed.

Whoa. A bed? Disorientation swirled around him. Where was his camp cot? The drafty shack? The snores of the Army of Freedom insurgents? Readiness to do violence flowed through him, making his limbs feel light and fast. Every sense went on high alert.

And then the smell of the pillow under his head struck him. Light. Soft. Vaguely sweet. *Like a woman.* And not just any woman. A feisty, feminine firecracker of a woman. What a tragedy that she'd taken the veil. She'd have made some lucky man incredibly happy.

He sat up and groaned at how stiff and sore he was when he tried to move this morning. Assuming it was still morning. The light coming in the window was pretty bright. Aah, the joys of a stim-pill hangover. He swung his feet to the floor and stood creakily, working out the kinks as he went. A quick watch check said it was noon. He'd slept nearly eleven hours. Not bad. Guys had been known to sleep for sixteen coming off a long no-sleep mission.

He dug into a pouch on his utility belt and came up with a handful of vitamins that he swallowed dry. The bitter taste fresh in his mouth, he headed down the hall for the communal bathroom, toothbrush in hand. While he was at it, he planned to grab a hot shower and a shave that would be an unexpected treat in the middle of a mission.

He emerged a little while later feeling like a new man. Now to find the world's most sexy and exasperating nun and make sure she didn't try anything suicidal today.

What the hell was he thinking? He had no business involving himself with her, either professionally or personally. And Lord knew he didn't need to have anything to do with a couple of orphaned kids. He'd been around the block plenty in this part of the world, and innocents got chewed up and spit out like bad candy. Frankly, his primary purpose in being here was much more pressing than stranded kids and the Flying Nun.

He ought to just pack up his gear and get out of here. Now that he knew where to find his targets, all he had to do was drive up into the jungle highlands and finish this arms deal. But as sure as he was standing here, he was going to collect one thoroughly annoying nun and go chasing after some snot-nosed brats. He didn't even like kids.

Irritated out of general principle, he stomped downstairs in search of the good sister. She was curled up on a decrepit sofa, her nose buried in a book, a pair of reading glasses perched on the end of her pert little nose. He noted with amusement that the lady was not reading a Bible, but rather a shoot-'em-up thriller novel.

She glanced up and smiled. "Hey there, Sleeping Beauty."

She thought he was beautiful, huh? Pleasure unfolded in his gut. Oh, for crying out loud. She was a freaking nun. It was downright creepy to continue being so attracted to her. He was beginning to wonder if something was wrong with him. He'd never had any strange or perverse sexual urges before, but this woman was seriously messing with his head.

"At least you didn't try to take off without me," he groused.

"Need a nice, hot cup of Juan Valdez's finest Colombian coffee to make you feel human?" she asked sympathetically.

He rolled his eyes, unwilling to be cajoled out of his rotten mood. But then she had to go around the front counter and pour him a cup of the stuff, and the rich strong scent of the steam wafting his way was too much for him. In spite of himself, he inhaled a long appreciative breath.

"How do you like it?" Elise asked over her shoulder.

His gaze raked down her back, taking in the slender curves and feminine proportions under the potato sack she called a dress. "Cream and sugar," he replied, distracted.

"How much of each?"

"About the color of your skin," he replied unthinkingly.

Her head whipped around and she stared over her shoulder at him, throwing him that wide-eyed look that always knocked him on his…well, that knocked him over. Her head swiveled back around and she finished preparing his coffee without comment. Cursing at himself, he watched her cautiously as she approached him and held out the chipped mug. He reached out to take the cup and his fingers brushed across hers. She drew a sharp breath and he jolted in alarm. He hadn't scared her, had he?

He looked up quickly, assessingly. Her pupils were huge and dark and her chest was rising and falling quickly. Dammit. Not afraid. She was something else entirely in response to his touch.

"Maybe we can find a priest for you when we get to Acuna," he murmured low.

"Why?"

"I'm betting you've got a whole lot of impure thoughts to confess. I can't even begin to imagine the number of Hail Marys you're going to have to recite."

Her laughter was sweet and untroubled and all but made the hair on his chest curl with need. He didn't see what was so funny, but a burning need to hear that sound again roared through him. "What's so funny?" he asked. "I'm only trying to look out for your eternal soul, here."

Head thrown back to reveal the soft column of her throat, she laughed again, this time hard enough that she probably wasn't aware of the hand she placed on his upper arm. But he was. Oh, how vividly he was. He froze, savoring the physical contact she'd initiated.

He was going to hell. Do not pass Go. Do not collect two hundred dollars. Straight to hellfire and brimstone for him. He was in total lust with a nun, and there wasn't a thing he could do about it.

He slugged down the hot coffee, uncaring that he was scorching his tongue and couldn't taste the fawn-colored brew.

"Need another one?" she asked, amused.

He shook his head as the caffeine did its magic in his veins, spreading alertness to his extremities and finally, hopefully, engaging his brain. "Too much caffeine after the stim pills isn't good for you."

"Like the stim pills are?" she retorted. She still looked on the verge of laughter at any moment.

"What's got you so chipper this morning?" he demanded.

"Well, you didn't abandon me here in this village, after all. We know where—" she broke off and glanced around quickly "—my church business can be concluded. And I've got a good feeling about our chances of success."

*Their* chances? As in the two of them together? He shouldn't like the sound of that, but darned if he didn't anyway. Right. Like a nun belonged in the middle of a dangerous and sensitive arms deal. He'd gone completely certifiable. Apparently, sexy nuns caused all his brains to fall out his left ear and explode.

Berating himself a hundred different ways for being an idiot, he followed her upstairs and collected her satchel of personal possessions and medical supplies. He placed her bag in the back of his Jeep and held the passenger door for her with a gallant wave of the hand. "Your chariot awaits you, Sister."

She smiled shyly and glided past him, peeking sidelong out of the corner of her eye at him. His pulse jumped and his body reacted eagerly in other ways that he didn't even want to think about. He slid behind the wheel and guided the vehicle west out of town.

"So. How long have you been a nun?" he asked, not taking his eyes off the uneven, two-lane asphalt road that passed for a highway in this part of the world.

"Not long. How long have you been an arms dealer?"

"Longer than I care to think about."

"Why do you say that?" she asked curiously.

He shrugged. "It's a job. But it takes you to crappy

corners of the world like this and forces you to work with some pretty unsavory characters."

She laughed. "Yup. That's me. Unsavory."

"Where are you from, anyway?"

"New York City."

"And your family? You're not white-bread Caucasian."

"I'm a little of everything. My mother is from the Phillipines. My father's father was black, his mother white. There's some Polynesian in there, too, but I'm not quite sure where in the family tree."

"Well, the result is lovely." He glanced over in time to catch the skeptical look she threw him. "What?" he demanded.

"I was just thinking that I'd hate to see who constitutes an unsavory character to an illegal arms dealer like you."

His gut tightened. He didn't blame her for having no respect for him, given what she thought his profession to be. But the negative judgment from her didn't sit well with him. If only she knew the truth

Frustrated, he changed the subject. "How did you find about these orphans you're hunting?"

"Father Ambrose—he's at Our Lady of Sacred Hope in Brooklyn—heard about them and asked me to come down here and get them."

"Who are they?" He couldn't imagine two random kids in the wilds of southern Colombia generating interest thousands of miles from their home.

Elise threw him an apologetic look. "The less you know, the better."

So. They *were* special in some way. He took a different tack with her. "Is it true that anything people say to you is privileged information you can't be forced to reveal?"

"Not only can people of the cloth not be forced to reveal confessions, they're obligated not to reveal anything."

Odd how she referred to priests and nuns as other people. She didn't include herself as one of them. "How long, exactly, have you been a nun?"

"I told you. Not long."

He smelled a rat. Why was she being so evasive with him? He could press her harder, but suspected she'd go all stubborn on him if he did. She might be a little thing, but she was a force of nature, that woman.

He drove for a while in silence. Then, he asked in spite of his resolution not to care, "How are you planning to get the kids out of Colombia?"

"The church has certain…understandings…with most governments. We are allowed to vouch for people and accompany them across international borders occasionally, and customs officials will ask no questions. Particularly in South America, which is so heavily Catholic, the Pope holds a fair bit of unofficial political clout."

Now there was an understatement. He had no doubt that the Pope could single-handedly topple a government down here if he really put his mind to it. Not that the Holy Father would, of course, without extreme provocation. Reluctantly, he admitted to himself that he was relieved the Catholic Church was involved with her orphans. The kids stood at least a chance of getting clear of this country's violence with that powerful organization behind them.

"Why did the church take an interest in these two children?" he tried.

"The church is in the business of protecting all innocents, particularly those who cannot protect themselves. Father Ambrose has brought dozens of orphans from war-torn places all around the world to the United States and found them permanent homes. He's a remarkable man."

"And you work for him?"

"Something like that."

Yet again, he sensed evasion, but he chose not to push. "Do you rescue orphans from war zones often?" The idea of her bombing around in other places as dangerous as this one twisted his gut with distress. An urge to go with her, to guard her from all danger took him by surprise. He was not in the business of protecting God's lambs, thank you, very much. At least not in the same way she was. He took a more…aggressive…approach to making the world safe for innocents like her and her kids.

"This is not my full-time work," she answered belatedly.

"What is? You aren't one of those terrifying teacher-nuns with a ruler and a thing for knuckles, are you?"

She rewarded him with another laugh that pealed across his skin like heavenly bells. "Good Lord, no. I'm a nurse. I work in emergency rooms, supplementing staff when they get short. But mostly I make house calls to people too poor or too illegal to seek health care through official means."

"Well, well. Aren't you just the crusading rebel?" he asked.

She shrugged. "I help people. I don't care who they are or where they come from. It's deeply satisfying work."

And for the first time, he saw the passionate zeal for service that he would expect from a nun. Disappointment coursed through him. Apparently, at some subconscious level, he'd been hoping she wasn't really committed to the whole nun thing and could be talked out of her habit and into his bed. What a cad he was! Appalled at himself, he fell silent.

They drove for several hours, the interior of the Jeep wreathed in grim silence. He pulled into a village in the late afternoon to fill up both his gas tank and the spare gas can strapped to the back of the Jeep. He was intrigued to see Elise reach up and slide the wimple off her hair as they pulled into town. It was a smart move. A nun would be noticed, but just some woman in the company of a man would be practically invisible in this traditionally male-dominated culture. Her hair fell in waves to her shoulders and looked as soft and strokable as a mink pelt.

"Hungry, Sister?" he asked, surprised at how hoarse his voice was all of a sudden..

"Yes. But I'll be okay if you want to press on. The sooner I get to those children, the better."

The road had been in worse condition than he'd been told to expect, probably the result of torrential rains the past few weeks, and they'd gotten a late start, compliments of his Sleeping Beauty routine. All of which added up to the fact that they weren't going to reach Acuna tonight. Regret that her orphans would have to wait another day for their rescue registered vaguely in his brain before he cut the feeling off cold. He was not going to get involved with her crazy project!

Except he was already involved, like it or not.

"It'll be tomorrow before we get there," he told her regretfully.

Deep alarm passed across her face. Afraid to be alone with him for the night, was she? He supposed he couldn't blame her. He'd been sniffing around her skirts like a rutting stag for far too long.

He sighed. "We can try to find a couple of beds for rent in this village, or we can drive until dark and camp in the jungle."

"Which is safer?"

"It's about a wash either way. We're in drug-cartel country, and saying the wrong word in a place like this will get you robbed at best and killed at worst. But the jungle has its own dangers, not the least of which being the wildlife and disease. And then, of course, the drug cartels are active out there, too. Your call."

She blinked, looking genuinely startled. "You're actually asking my opinion on something?" she blurted.

"I'm not that bad," he protested.

"Hah."

"Hey!"

"The jungle."

"Excuse me?" He had the worst time trying to follow her train of thought sometimes.

"I vote for continuing on and spending the night in the jungle. We'll be less visible. Less rumors will circulate about us. A nun and an arms dealer traveling together are bound to cause a bit of a sensation."

He grunted. True. And both of them would benefit by staying as low under the local drug lords' radars as possible. He was still convinced the kids she was here to rescue were far from average, anonymous orphans.

After ordering her quietly to stay in the car and out of sight, he walked next door to top off his store of supplies. He wasn't the kind of man who usually had trouble in places like this—apparently his decades of training in hand-to-hand fighting showed through in the way he carried himself—but he wasn't about to take any chances with Elise's safety.

They headed out as the sun descended slowly into the west. Thankfully, the jungle was still thick enough to block it from his eyes for the most part. Now and then, clear patches were starting to appear where areas of jungle had been slashed and burned to make way for food crops or the insanely valuable coca plants that were the primary source of income—and violence—in this region.

They had about a half hour of twilight left before full dark when he started looking for a likely place to pull off the road and make camp. In a few minutes he found what he sought. Relatively dry land on the side of a mountain, enough underbrush to hide a vehicle, but enough old-growth forest on the hillside above to allow for a decent clearing in which to pitch a tent, and a fast-running stream nearby.

He'd been avoiding thinking about the fact that he only had one tent. Buying a second one would've drawn too much attention to Elise, and frankly, it would've signaled far too deep a commitment to helping her. Everything between them was still temporary, and he planned to keep it that way.

With quick efficiency, he unloaded the supplies they would need. Elise carried the light gear up the hillside while he hid the Jeep and then followed her carrying the heavy stuff. He approved of the tiny clearing she'd stopped in and helped her clear a patch of ground down to the dirt. The critters that lived on the floor of this jungle were emphatically not the kind a person wanted to have join them in their tent in the middle of the night. Dried leaves hid everything from army ants to deadly snakes out here.

"You act like you've done this before," he commented.

Unaccountably, pain flashed across her face. He lurched forward with an impulse to put his arms around her and comfort her. But then she looked up at him and the grief raging in her gaze froze him in place.

"What's wrong?" he asked quickly.

"I used to do this with my parents—" Her voice cracked. She cleared her throat and then mumbled, "It has been a long time…thought it wouldn't be this bad… too many memories…"

He knew precisely how memories of lost friends and colleagues could haunt a soul. It was one of the hazards of his profession. People you loved died. He waited for her to say more, but she fell silent, lost in tragic contemplation. Sadly, he knew the cure for that. You had to pick yourself up and go on. They were dead, you were not. You went on living. But his heart ached for her loss anyway.

He passed her a collapsible bucket. "Go fetch water. I'll put up the tent and get a fire started."

She nodded and headed off into the trees toward the sound of cheerfully bubbling water.

By the time he'd finished building the entire camp, Elise still hadn't returned with the water. Concerned, he headed out after her. The last remnants of the gloaming filtered down through the canopy overhead and he made out mostly gray shapes and shadows. The sound of the little stream grew louder, and he slowed down, approaching with caution. Crouching, he eased forward on battle alert. The night sounds around him gave no indication that other predators prowled the night, but he took no chances, nonetheless.

The way his stomach jumped with nervous anxiety was a nasty surprise. She was just a nun. An asset to be looked after. There was no reason whatsoever for him to be personally concerned about her. Wasn't her safety in God's hands, anyway?

Right. And that was why the butterflies in his stomach refused to settle down despite all the calming exercises he ran through in his mind. He'd been in gunfights and ambushed, his life put in extreme danger a hundred times, and always been cool as a cucumber. But here he was all alone, sweating bullets that one small female had somehow managed to get herself into trouble.

He crept around a giant fern and caught sight of a movement ahead. He froze. Very slowly, he drew his pistol. Inch by inch, he moved closer to get a better view. Something light moved against a backdrop of black, crouching down and then rising up again.

A faint groan reached his ears and his pulse shot up unpleasantly. Was that Elise? Was she in pain? Every nerve screamed at him to bolt forward and save her. Only his long years of training, and the sure and certain knowledge that his stupidity would get her killed faster than anything else out here, gave him the discipline to hold his position.

Another slow step forward. And another.

The shape crouched and rose again, this time half-turning toward him.

Stunned, he stared as he finally made out exactly what he was seeing. Elise was taking a bath. Well, not a bath, exactly. She'd stripped naked and was using a washcloth to scoop up water and stream it down over her glorious body. Her spine was outlined by a long, tantalizing trail of soapsuds that disappeared into the crevice of her buttocks. The shape of her behind captured his gaze; the way it curved into her thighs made his breath catch in his throat.

She scooped up a handful of water and held her arms up overhead. The water ran down her slender arms, washing a mound of suds into the valley between breasts that were arguably the most perfect he'd ever seen. His breath stopped altogether. Her head was thrown back, her eyes closed in ecstasy, her profile as pure as the clear water dripping onto her collarbones.

As the night cooled rapidly around him, his body raged with fire to rival the searing heat of this tropical climate. This was not lust. It wasn't even need. It was a pull of instinct so visceral, so overwhelming, he didn't even know how to think past it, let alone how to control it.

It shouldn't shock him that a nun was also a woman, but he was absolutely stunned that she was such a sensual creature beneath all those clothes designed to make her as unattractive as possible.

Elise groaned again, and there was no mistaking the sound of pleasure. It vibrated through him with the force of an earthquake. He absolutely had to hear her make that sound again. He'd give up his eternal soul to be the one to cause her to make that sound.

He took an aggressive step forward and a twig snapped underfoot. Elise's eyes popped open and he froze in horror in the act of stalking her.

"Who's there?" she called out nervously.

Good God, almighty. He was voyeuristically intruding upon the private bath of a nun. N. U. N. Nun. He'd turned into a freaking pervert. He whirled violently to put his back to her and called over his shoulder, "It's me. I was worried about you. Everything okay?"

The sounds of frantic movement came from behind him. She had to be snatching up a towel and holding it across her body like an inadequate shield. "Uh, yes." She sounded out of breath, no doubt racing to yank on her clothes. Covering herself in panic. Please, God, let her not realize he'd seen her enjoying her bath like that. She'd be too humiliated to ever look him in the eye again.

For all the money in the world he wouldn't give up having seen her naked in the jungle with water and soap-suds running down her body like a blessing. But neither did he want to lose the easy familiarity between them.

She spoke breathlessly from just behind him. "The water was so cool and refreshing looking, I couldn't resist. I took a little sponge bath. I'm sorry if I worried you."

Huh. Worry didn't quite describe what she'd done to him. An image of her burned in his mind as brightly as the sun, and no power on earth was removing that from his head anytime soon.

"Did you enjoy it?" he choked out as she moved up beside him. He risked glancing at her out of the corner of his eye. The potato sack was firmly back in place. But when he looked at her now, all he saw was silky skin and womanly curves. Sex. Mind-blowing sex. Pleasure that transcended mere mortal intensity.

He must've made a sound because she glanced at him in concern. "Are you okay?"

"Yes. No. Uh, yes."

"Which is it?" She stopped and turned to face him, her smile glowing in the dark like a beacon calling him home.

"I'm fine."

A frown creased her forehead, as if she was suddenly questioning exactly what he'd seen. He blurted quickly, "Let me take that bucket of water from you. I've got purification tablets for it back in camp. It'll taste like iodine, but it'll be safe to drink in an hour."

She replied dryly, "Yes, I'm familiar with how water purification tablets work."

"Of course you are. We can heat some of the water up and reconstitute the freeze-dried food I've got. But you know how that works, too—" He broke off as her grin widened. He was babbling. Actually *babbling*.

"You sure you're okay?" she asked.

"Yes, I'm sure," he snapped. "I'm fine." He was so *not* fine. He was a mess. He was in total, no-holds-barred lust with this woman.

She eyed him suspiciously. Apparently, another typically nunlike trait she had in abundance was knowing when people weren't being truthful with her. Swearing up a blue storm under his breath, he led her back to camp and went about heating water and making them both dinner— if reconstituted chili mac and freeze-dried strawberry ice cream could rightly be called dinner.

He let the fire burn down to a glowing pile of embers and Elise seemed content to sit thoughtfully beside it and watch it die.

Finally, he muttered, "We'd better call it a night. We've got a long day ahead of us tomorrow."

She looked up quickly. "I thought you said we'd reach Acuna my midmorning."

"We will. But once we collect your precious cargo, we've got to put as much distance between Acuna and ourselves as we can before we stop. Just to be safe."

He was *not* doing this. He was not helping her collect her blessed orphans! He had other fish to fry, more important fish. But as sure as he was sitting here, he was delaying his own mission to help her with hers. If his boss got wind of this, he was going to be toast. Burned to a crisp, in fact.

"Right. Safe." She sounded skeptical about achieving that state anywhere in this country. Smart girl. Her safety around him was a much more precarious thing than he cared to admit, but he was walking a razor's edge between lust and honor right now.

He unzipped the tent flap and held it up for her. "Crawl in."

He tried not to watch her pert little derriere as she crawled through the low opening. He really tried. But the image of it naked and wet and squeezable just wouldn't go away. Swearing under his breath, he reached for the zipper.

"Hey. Aren't you going to join me?"

Oh, Lord. "No. I'm going to sleep out here."

"That's crazy."

Her pronouncement shocked him out of the haze fogging his brain function. "I beg your pardon?" he asked blankly.

"This is Colombia. Home of every poisonous insect and snake in creation. And they all love warmth at night. If you sleep out there, you'll have a veritable zoo crawling all over you by morning. It's unsafe to sleep directly on the ground."

He snorted and refrained from telling her about the first time he'd tied himself into a tree to sleep during a mission in this region and woken up with a deadly eyelash viper curled peacefully asleep in his lap the next morning. He'd sweated for three hours before the damned thing finally woke up and meandered off into the tree branches.

She had a point. This wasn't an ideal place to spend a night without some sort of protection from the wildlife. But no way was he spending the night a foot away from her without laying his hands on her. He might be disciplined, but she was too much temptation for him.

"I'll be okay out here," he replied stiffly.

"Don't be an idiot. Get in here."

"No."

"Do I have to come out there and get you?"

His lips twitched. That drill-sergeant tone of voice was just cute coming from all five-foot-two-fluffy-kitten of her.

"Go to sleep, Elise."

"Okay."

His brows slammed together. Since when did she give up so easily? She was up to something. Sure enough, the zipper zinged in a few moments and the flap opened. "Move over," she announced.

"Why?"

"I'm coming out."

"Forget to make a pit stop before bedtime?"

"Nope."

He started as a wad of down-filled sleeping bag bulged

through the tent opening. "What are you doing?" he demanded.

"Coming out to sleep with you."

"Oh, no you don't—" he started.

She cut him off. "If it's good enough for you, it's good enough for me. I'm not sleeping in the tent unless you do."

He cringed at the note of obstinate finality in her voice. "This is madness."

"Actually," she replied blithely, "it's blackmail. If you want me to get eaten alive out here, so be it. Otherwise, we're both going inside and getting a decent, safe night's sleep."

His gaze narrowed. He did not appreciate blackmail. Not from his clients and not from her.

No doubt to emphasize her point, she swatted at her arm. "I swear. The mosquitoes out here are the size of hummingbirds."

The idea of her tender skin red and puffy with bug bites made his gut twist. Oh, she was good, all right. He scowled at her. "I didn't know nuns were allowed to fight so dirty."

Her chuckle was low and sexy. "You have no idea."

Reluctantly, he capitulated, gesturing for her to get back inside the tent and take her sleeping bag with her. At least she had the good grace not to gloat as he crawled in beside her. Furious with himself for giving in and terrified at how much further he'd weaken tonight, he stretched out on top of his sleeping bag, tense.

The light scent of her body wash wafted over him and he seriously regretted caving in to her demands. He'd wait until she fell asleep, and then he'd sneak outside to spend the night.

Except she seemed to have no interest in sleeping. He lay there, board stiff, listening to her breathing not settling down into the rhythms of sleep. Finally, he broke the silence. "Something on your mind, Sister?"

"Why do you ask?"

"You should have been asleep a while ago."

"Why are you still awake? Guilty conscience?"

Crap. Did she know he'd seen her taking that bath? "Uh, no. Why do you say that?" he asked cautiously.

"What else would keep a man awake after a long day?"

"I slept late this morning. What's your excuse? Is your conscience bugging you, perchance?"

She sighed quietly. "Actually, it is. I'm afraid I'm not being a very good nun."

If, by that, she meant she was too damned tempting for her own good, he had to agree. "Far be it from me to judge such a thing," he commented. "It's between you and God."

She started to snort, but then the sound cut off short. Did the nun have a small problem with God at the moment? Was he tempting her? He supposed he should feel bad about that. Instead, a surge of fierce joy surged in his gut. But then, he was already going to hell. No need to feel guilty about adding to his long list of sins. Right?

He tossed and turned for a while longer, waiting for her to go to sleep. But instead, he woke abruptly some time later. The night was deep and mostly silent around him. What had woken him like that? He trusted his instincts completely. Some threat had registered on his subconscious mind.

And then he registered the warm weight slithering across his chest. His fingers groped for the knife beside his sleeping bag. The weight moved slightly and he froze. Not a snake. An arm. Elise's arm. She must've reached across him and that had woken him. He relaxed beneath it, grinning. That's what he got for talking about snakes right before going to sleep.

But then another weight moved across his thighs. Crud! The nun had thrown a leg over him, too. In fact, she was all but lying on top of him. She'd be mortified if she woke up and found them sprawled together like this. In the interest of sparing her modesty, he started to ease out from beneath her. But both arm and leg tightened immediately. He moved even more slowly, but all he accomplished was making her slide her body more fully on top of his.

A soft breast pressed against his chest, its resilient texture causing all kinds of havoc with his body. A lock of her hair tickled his neck and he reached up carefully to lift it aside. Except the woman apparently had nerves in her hair and stirred at his touch.

She mumbled inarticulately and lifted her head. He turned his head to the side to gaze at her, but it was too dark to make out her features and see if she was fully awake.

As he watched, she drew closer to him. What was she doing? He froze, stunned. For all the world it looked as if she was about to—

—she kissed him!

Her mouth was soft and warm against his stunned lips. It moved lightly, butterfly delicate against his mouth. A groan rose in his throat, but he choked it off lest he wake her from whatever dream gripped her.

"Mmm," she murmured as if he were the most delicious dessert she'd ever sampled.

Amen to that. She tasted like cream and honey. He moved his mouth ever so slightly against hers, carefully sampling the forbidden fruit. Aah, how easy the fall into temptation was. She voiced the groan of pleasure he was feeling and her entire body moved sinuously against his. Her hand slid up his chest and across his collarbone to his right ear, cupping his neck. Her fingertips teased his earlobe and urged him deeper into the kiss. He obliged, half turning beneath her, his arms coming up around her.

She felt like heaven in his arms. Woman with a capital W. Everything he'd ever dreamed of finding in a girl. She was as soft and sweet as she was strong and fierce. Her mouth opened against his and her tongue traced his lips lightly. In turn, he caught her lower lip between his teeth and scored its plump juiciness until she moaned and pressed her entire body forward against his.

The thin cotton camisole beneath his palms did nothing to protect her from his need. His fingers slipped under the edge of the garment and he inhaled in sharp pleasure at the feel of her silken skin beneath his palms. In turn, her hands crept around the back of his neck, pulling his head down more fully into their kiss.

He surged up over her, rolling her onto her back and taking command of the kiss, exploring her mouth openly now, savoring the taste of her, the way her small perfect teeth ran across his tongue, the way her clever tongue teased his, inviting him deeper into her. His hand slid around her rib cage to cup the fullness of a breast, lightly molding the flesh to his touch. His thumb rubbed once, twice, across a proud bud. She arched up into the caress, as responsive and sensual as he'd guessed she would be beneath those boring clothes.

Those religious clothes.

Nun.

Holy crap.

He froze in the act of reaching for her camisole hem to take it off. Eased his hand away from her hip by slow degrees. Withdrew his tongue carefully from her mouth. Lifted his lips—reluctantly—away from hers. He settled her bowed body back ever so gently to her sleeping bag and pushed up onto an elbow as he lifted his body off of hers.

He glanced at her face and froze in shock so profound that his mind went completely blank.

*She was awake.*

Her gaze, dark and unfathomable, met his.

She hadn't been dreaming through that incendiary kiss? What did it mean? What was he supposed to do now?

# Chapter 5

*Okay, so that pretty much blew the whole nun cover.* And the whole aversion to getting involved with a criminal thing.

Shock poured through Elise, but for the life of her, she couldn't summon a single ounce of regret that she'd kissed him like that. That had been arguably the best kiss she'd ever experienced, and she had a feeling he'd just been getting going. What would it be like if he hadn't stopped? If he hadn't remembered that she was a nun and off-limits? If he'd finished weaving the magic on her body and soul that he'd started so spectacularly?

His mouth opened. No doubt he was going to apologize. Beat himself up like crazy for crossing the line with her. Regret slammed into her. But not regret that she'd kissed him. Oh, no. She only regretted making him feel bad about himself.

She pressed her fingertips against his lips to halt the

apology, to halt the self-recriminations. She opened her own mouth to tell him it was all right. That it was her fault. That she'd known full well what she was doing when she'd crawled all over him like that and tempted him into kissing her.

But before the words could cross her lips, a series of metallic clicks rattled all around the tent.

Drago's eyes popped wide open in alarm and chagrin, but she didn't need the expression to know that they were in deep, deep trouble. She hadn't worked the mean streets of New York's toughest neighborhoods for nothing. Those were safeties clicking off a whole bunch of weapons.

"Let me go out first. They're less likely to shoot me on sight," she murmured as the tent zipper started to unzip. She reached quickly for her wimple and tucked it behind her ears. He shoved her sweater at her and she donned it quickly, her fingers fumbling frantically at the buttons. The muzzle of a double-barreled shotgun poked through the opening in the nylon fabric.

She spoke calmly, "Good evening, gentlemen. I am a nun and unarmed. I'm getting dressed as we speak and will be right out to speak with you. I'm so glad you found me."

Drago nodded briefly beside her as he pulled a T-shirt over his head. He'd worn pants to sleep in, but she doubted he'd have time to put on his hiking boots before their visitors forced them outside. She reached into his pack without asking and snagged his sweatpants. Awkwardly, she dragged them on and headed for the tent door on her hands and knees. Heart in her throat, she crawled outside.

The men surrounding her looked much like Enrique and his men had—hard and violent. They reacted in surprise to her wimple, and thankfully didn't shoot her on sight. She silently blessed Father Ambrose for suggesting the nun masquerade.

"So. The rumors are true. A *loco* nun is running around the jungle," one of the men commented.

She eyed him in particular. He held himself like a leader. She nodded at him and rose slowly to her feet, her hands held carefully in sight and away from her sides. "That's correct. To whom do I have the pleasure of speaking tonight?"

The weapons jerked as Drago appeared in the tent opening.

"Who's this?" the leader of the group exclaimed.

"He's my driver," she explained.

Drago stood up beside her, his hands clasped behind his neck without the other men having to tell him to do it. "I am *not* her driver. I am a businessman. And she is the most annoying creature on the planet. She hitched a ride with me and wouldn't take no for an answer." He shrugged in obvious frustration. "How do you say no to a nun, for God's sake?"

Inexplicably, the men around her relaxed at his explanation. Yet again, he'd judged these men better than her and said exactly the right thing to diffuse the tension. Who was he? Despite his business, she was more convinced than ever there was more to Drago than met the eye.

"And who might you be?" the leader asked.

"Drago Cantori," he announced.

"The arms dealer?"

"Who's asking?" Drago retorted.

"Enrique told us you'd be coming this way. He didn't say anything about a nun, though."

Yikes! This guy was the leader of the Army of Freedom? She gulped as Drago snorted. "I tried to ditch her, but she's as tenacious as a tick. Pesky little thing. But she cooks a mean stuffed *arepa*."

Yet again, it was her cooking skill that evoked real interest in these men. Was that all they thought women were good for? Cooking? Sheesh.

"Are you Raoul?" Drago asked.

"No." The leader laughed. "But I will take you to him. He is most interested in having a conversation with you. You two make business together, eh?"

"The sooner the better," Drago replied with unmistakable eagerness.

She scowled. All hot and bothered to make a big arms deal, was he? If it wouldn't have screwed up her own mission and gotten her killed, she'd have run interference on his arms dealing so fast his head would spin. A few words to the right people questioning the quality of his goods, a dropped hint that he'd welched on deals before, and he'd be out of business in this part of the world.

"Come with us," the patrol leader ordered.

"I need my bag," she blurted. Everyone's attention riveted on her. Drat. And she'd been doing such a good job of being invisible. "It's got all my medical supplies in it," she explained hastily.

The leader gestured to one of his men, who ducked into the tent and emerged a moment later with her canvas satchel. The guy shoved it into her arms. Not going to carry the lady's bag for her, was he? Mentally sniffing at his lack of manners, she took the precious bag of first-aid supplies.

"What about the tent?" she asked.

"Leave it. You won't need it where we're going."

She didn't like the sound of that. They were being treated like prisoners and that couldn't possibly be a good thing.

"Don't cause trouble," Drago muttered under his breath in English.

She subsided, falling in meekly beside him as the group tromped down the hill toward the road and their Jeep. She'd bet the insurgents didn't leave that behind.

As they approached the road, a rustle in the trees was her only warning before deafening gunfire exploded around them.

Drago's response was lightning fast. He threw an arm around her shoulders and threw her to the ground, his big body crushing hers. Damp leaves and dirt mashed against her face as bright flashes lit the night around them and their captors returned fire.

"Can you shoot a gun?" Drago asked urgently in her ear.

"Yes."

He rolled off of her fast. "Stay low. This way."

She mimicked his belly-on-the-ground crawl over to a massive fallen log. He rolled to a sitting position in its shadow and she did the same. He pressed something cold and metal and heavy into her hand. A pistol.

"Fourteen rounds," he bit out.

"Who am I supposed to shoot at?"

"Anyone who moves." He pointed with his own hand-gun over the log toward the road. "The guys who found us first are Army of Freedom. Whoever jumped them is government or bandits. Either way, the second group is the bad guys."

She frowned. The Colombian government wasn't technically bad. At least not everyone within it. The army was genuinely trying to contain the drug trade and the violence, to weed out men like Valdiron Garza who'd used their government positions for self-aggrandizement and corruption. But reforms were expensive and slow. When a man's children were starving, he wasn't generally inclined to be patient…or give a damn for the legality of a rich cash crop.

Drago popped up beside her, took a moment to sight a target and squeezed off two shots. As he ducked back down, he ordered, "Watch my back."

That she could do. She scanned the jungle above them for movement of any kind. It was hard to concentrate. She kept flinching as each new volley of gunfire erupted. But then she spotted a shadow creeping down toward them. Vividly aware of her limited ammunition, she took careful aim before firing. A cry in the trees indicated she'd hit her man. The weapon kicked hard in her hand, and she steadied it before taking a second shot at the target. The shadow toppled over.

She picked up her scan of the woods for more targets. There. Off to the right. Just coming out of the trees. The guy had a rifle raised to his shoulder and it was aimed right at Drago's back! She fired twice in quick succession and was gratified to see the man drop like a stone.

The gunfire faded into silence as fast as it had broken out.

Drago dropped back down beside her and ejected a clip from his pistol. He slammed in another one. "How are you doing for ammo?"

"Ten shots left," she replied tersely.

He nodded. They waited together, but silence stretched out around them.

"All clear," someone shouted.

She started to get up, but a hard hand on her arm yanked her back down. "Wait," he mouthed.

Sure enough, as the Army of Freedom men began to rise from their hiding places, another volley of gunfire broke out. Drago peeked up over the log and took a half-dozen more careful shots. She had to admit, the guy was cool under fire. He took his time and didn't spray shots wildly into the night. And given the ease with which he handled that gun, she'd bet every shot was hitting its target.

Blessedly, the hillside above them remained quiet and undisturbed.

Finally, several minutes later, another all clear was called out. And this time Drago nodded to her. "Stay here. I'll go confirm your kills."

She blinked, startled. Her kills? It dawned on her that she'd shot two men. Her hands started to shake, and then her knees. She'd *shot* two men. How on earth was she going to explain that and still maintain her cover as a nun? In her panic, had she just blown the whole rescue?

She replayed the movements in the jungle above her in her mind's eye. No, if she hadn't shot those men, they'd have killed her and Drago. It had been a kill or be killed scenario. But still. She was supposed to be a nun. They didn't kill people, did they? She was pretty sure the "Thou shalt not kill" clause was nonnegotiable.

She swore under her breath.

Drago slid back down the hill to her position. "Good shooting," he commented. "Where'd you learn to do that?"

She couldn't very well tell him that gang members in various New York neighborhoods had shown her how to handle a weapon and urged her to pack a piece for her own safety. The funny bit had been that they'd all been trying to protect her from each other. As long as she'd been the lady with the medical kit who'd treated all of them impartially and without questions, she'd been safe in the middle of the gang wars.

She shrugged and took the hand he held down to her.

Their palms met and memory of that steamy kiss in the tent slammed through her.

Drago lifted her to her feet and didn't release her hand. Instead, he tugged her nearer, murmuring under his breath, "A nun who kisses like she wants more and kills a man without hesitation? Who are you?"

"Aah. There you are," a male voice called out from behind them. "Nice shooting, Drago. Obviously you are familiar with your products, amigo."

Drago released her hand as the leader of the rebel patrol climbed toward them, and she stumbled back, abjectly relieved.

"You have eyes in the back of your head?" the rebel leader asked. "You are very fast, indeed, to have shot those men in front of you and the ones behind you."

Elise's eyes opened wide in dismay. No way would these guys believe a nun had killed a couple of men. Her cover was so blown.

Drago shrugged modestly beside her. "I've been in this business a few years. You learn things here and there. Develop a sixth sense for the man behind you."

He was taking credit for her kills? Now, why would he do that? Was there more to this arms dealer than met the eye? Did he actually have a conscience? She glanced up at him in gratitude. He ignored her, his jaw hard.

"I would like to see how fast you are, sometime," the leader speculated.

"No, you wouldn't," Drago replied grimly. "I only draw my weapon to kill. And you don't want to be on the receiving end of my shooting. I never miss."

The rebel glanced around the clearing reluctantly. "So I see. I must admit, we'd have been in trouble without your gun. You dropped almost half those soldiers by yourself."

Elise glanced up at Drago, startled. He'd killed half the

bandits on his own? And he was demanding to know who *she* was? Who was *he?*

A man jogged up to the apparent leader. "All the soldiers are dead and we stripped the useful gear. But someone is calling them on the radio We should leave soon before backup arrives."

The report galvanized the party. They all took off running down the hill toward their vehicles.

"Let's go. Raoul will be most interested to hear about this little ambush."

"Were the attackers Colombian Army?" Drago asked tersely.

"Aye."

"Their intel is good if they knew I was coming to see you."

The rebel leader threw him a look of sharp speculation. Yet again, Elise was impressed by Drago's savvy. By implying that the ambush had been about him, he'd just exponentially raised his status and importance in the eyes of the rebels.

Elise followed Drago down the hill thoughtfully. He seemed content to let the rebels herd them into the backseat of their Jeep. Casually, he tossed the keys to one of their captors.

As the vehicle bumped down the road, she'd have given anything to snuggle up against his big, warm body. Shock from the earlier attack was setting in, and she felt terrible. She'd killed two men. Did they have wives? Kids? What were their names?

"Don't think about it," Drago muttered to her in English.

She threw him an anguished look.

His hand crept surreptitiously across the space between them and captured her fingers in his. It was a small comfort, but she was immensely grateful for it. It had been a long time since anyone had offered a shoulder to lean on. Not since Father Ambrose had climbed on that bridge with her and shown her how much she had to offer her fellow man. How, in spite of all she'd lost, she still had so much to live for.

Ever since, she'd always been the one lending others the strength she'd found within herself that cold night. In fact, she'd been nearly manic about it. As if she couldn't ever pay back her debt to society. *Or the debt to her parents.* The thought was a hot blade of agony slicing through her gut. She shied away violently from that train of thought. And now she had two more deaths to add to her conscience.

Drago's fingers tightened on hers as though he sensed her disquiet. Perceptive man. Too perceptive. How on earth was she going to answer his questions when they finally got a moment to themselves to talk? She wanted worse than anything to tell him she wasn't a nun. But did she dare trust him with that secret? Her life and the lives of the children she was here to save might very well ride on it. No matter how badly she wanted to kiss him again, to see where it took the two of them, she dared not tell. At the end of the day, she couldn't trust a man like him.

But as sure as she was sitting here, he was going to kiss her again. She'd been lucky this time that they'd been interrupted. If being kidnapped by armed insurgents and ambushed and nearly killed by the Army could be termed luck.

How on earth was she going to resist him next time?

# Chapter 6

When they got to wherever they were going, he would corner Elise and do whatever it took to get the truth out of her. She was no more a nun than he was an actual arms dealer. She was, however, a hell of a woman. She hadn't balked when he'd put a gun in her hands, hadn't hesitated to kill when she had to, hadn't gotten all hysterical about it after the fact. Levelheaded, she was. Cool under pressure. The kind of person he could trust with his life.

Except for the fact that she was lying her ass off about the whole nun thing.

If she really was here to rescue some kids, he supposed he could see the logic of the ruse. This wasn't exactly a safe corner of the world for a woman alone. But why was she here at all? Why hadn't a mercenary been sent to retrieve the kids? Or at least someone better suited to the dangers of this place? Someone like him.

Whoa. Strike that. He wasn't about to get into the business of hauling children out of the middle of a brush war. He had a job to do, and that was his first—*and only*—priority. He swore mentally. Then why was he holding hands with the not-nun and sitting here frantically trying to figure out a plausible explanation for her presence that the senior leadership of the Army of Freedom would buy?

The Jeep pulled into a village as dawn started to lighten the sky. He climbed out of the vehicle and went around to help Elise out. She took his hand for the long step down, and he didn't release it when she was standing beside him. Rather, he tucked it under his arm, wrapping her fingers around his elbow.

Hopefully, she understood he was signaling to the rebels that she was under his protection. Thankfully, she didn't balk. In fact, she leaned in close to him as if she drew strength from him. All the better. If only she meant it for real.

They were led into a cantina that looked like just about every other bar in this part of the world. It was dark and the sprinkling of men inside were hard and mean. He and Elise were led to a cramped room in the back and deposited at the table with an admonition to wait for Raoul, the Army of Freedom's leader, to arrive. The other men stepped back out into the main bar and yelled for breakfast.

He leaned over to murmur in English, "We need to talk."

She made a noncommittal sound.

"Just follow my lead with these guys, okay?"

She countered, "Are we prisoners?"

"Not exactly. They desperately want to do business with me, but they don't trust anyone, including me. Helping them out in that fight last night went a long way toward proving myself, but you've thrown them for a loop."

"I'm sorry." But then she smiled a little. "Although, if I'm messing up your arms deal, I'm not actually sorry about that."

He replied tightly, "There's more going on here than meets the eye. I need you to trust me and not fight me."

He winced as she sat back and studied him speculatively. Why did she have to be so darned quick on the uptake? She was bound to read all kinds of things into that cryptic comment. But he couldn't tell her any more. Hell, he shouldn't have told her that much. However, she was just cussed enough to interfere in his arms deal if she thought she was doing the right thing.

"I need to get out of here," she said quietly. "Time's a-wasting."

"Be patient. These guys don't respond well to being pushed. I'll do my best to cut us loose as soon as possible."

Us? Why had that word slipped out of his mouth? Now that he'd made contact with the Army of Freedom's top brass, albeit sooner than he'd planned, he couldn't very well leave them to go fetch a pair of orphans. But he hated the idea of letting her proceed on her own. Far too many things could go wrong for her. He swore at himself; he had no choice. Duty came first.

"Just get me out of here and we'll call it good." Hearing her voice his exact thought aloud ticked him off for some reason he couldn't put his finger on.

"I'm not abandoning you among these people," he snapped. "Let alone the danger from these guys, you saw those soldiers who jumped them last night. This area is beyond risky. What on earth possessed you to come down here, anyway?"

"I gave my word."

And therein lay the rub. He could understand that, even grudgingly respect it. His word was his bond, as well.

"Next time, think more carefully before you promise to do something for someone, eh?"

She smiled sadly at him. "I had no illusions about what I was getting myself into. I knew how dangerous this trip would be."

And she'd still come? "Are you suicidal?" he blurted. Surely, yet another pair of kids without parents weren't worth dying over. And yet…whether he liked it or not, he felt the same protective tug she did when he thought of innocent children stranded in the middle of the violence all around him.

"I'm not suicidal anymore. I'm doing this because I owed Father Ambrose a favor."

Not anymore? Now what did that mean? Quick alarm flooded him. The idea of her taking herself out of this world appalled him. She was too vibrant, too *alive* to end her life prematurely. "What you're doing goes way beyond a simple favor. It's…" He didn't know what. But no debt could be so big that she should throw away her life to repay it.

She laid a light hand on his arm and he about jumped out of his skin. His entire body went hypersensitive from just that simple touch. She said, "It's my choice. My responsibility. I appreciate everything you've done for me. But really. This is my problem. Not yours."

He leaned forward and hissed, "I choose to make it my problem, so get over it." As the words left his mouth, he knew them to be incontrovertibly true. But why? He *knew* better. Elise and those kids were emphatically not his job. But she needed his help, and he was apparently pathologically incapable of turning away from her need.

Maybe he was losing the handle. It was a known phenomenon in his line of work. Sometimes operators like him hit an emotional wall and just couldn't go on with their profession anymore. It wasn't that they wimped out. It was as if they just ran out of gas. Their souls were empty and they had no more left to give. Was that happening to him?

He looked up and caught her scowling at him, but then confusion entered her gaze. Curiosity.

"Don't ask," he warned her with a cautionary glance toward the main room. He looked back at her, irritated, and his gaze drifted down to her mouth.

"I won't ask if you won't," she retorted tartly.

Huh. If she thought she was getting out of explaining that smoking-hot kiss to him, she had another think coming. As soon as they were alone, she would tell him exactly who she was. Right before she kissed him like that again.

"I think you should tell these men why you're here," he said thoughtfully.

She lurched in her seat. "Not a chance!" she exclaimed under her breath.

"Why not? They'll respect your desire to save innocent children. Protecting the young is a universal value. With very few exceptions, people look out for them."

She gritted out so low he barely heard her, "They're not innocents."

"Come again?"

"Well, they are. But their family is not."

Ah ha. So he'd been right after all. They weren't just some random kids who'd come to the attention of some random priest. He asked once more, "Who are they?"

She shook her head. "Can't tell you."

He thought back to his in-briefings before he'd headed down here. Who could they be? What high profile individuals had died in this area recently— His brain screeched to an appalled halt.

"They're not the Gar—"

"Hush." She cut him off sharply, looking panicked.

*Sweet Mother of God.* "You have *got* to be kidding. Are you insane?" he demanded.

"Keep your voice down," she ordered.

"You *are* insane. Do you have any idea—"

"I know exactly who they are. Who he was."

"No, you don't. He—"

"—murdered my parents."

Ted fell back in his chair, stunned. Valdiron Garza had murdered her parents, and she was still here to rescue his kids? Hell. Maybe she was a nun, after all. What other explanation was there for her madness if she thought she could rescue that man's children all by herself?

"This isn't about vengeance, is it?"

Her eyes widened in genuine horror. Nope. Not a revenge thing, then. He was relieved to know that, at least. But it brought him back to his original question. Why in the world would she attempt to rescue the children of the man who'd killed her parents? And knowing Garza, the man who'd probably tortured her parents first?

"I swear, woman. The first moment we are truly alone, you've got a whole lot of explaining to do."

Right. Like she was sticking around to face that little interrogation. Like it or not, she had to ditch Drago. And fast. Before he got a chance to corner her and force answers out of her. As desperately as she'd love to stay with him and to let him help her and the kids get out of Colombia alive, she dared not. He was getting far too close to truths she simply wasn't ready to talk about. Not with anyone.

It turned out to be ridiculously easy to escape. The rebels took Drago somewhere more private to talk to the big kahuna, that Raoul guy. Once everyone had cleared out of the cantina, she asked the bartender for a restroom and was shown to an unspeakably bad-smelling little closet with an ancient, high-tank toilet. Thankfully, it had a window, and even more thankfully, it was open.

She slipped out through the opening and dropped to the ground in a fetid alley. Slipping off her wimple and stuffing it in the pocket of her sweater, she walked away from the bar. The village wasn't large, and her options were limited. She had no money, no identification, no transportation, and no idea where she was.

The first order of business, though, was to put some distance between herself and the rebels, not to mention Drago. Sticking to the back of the low buildings, she made her way to the other end of town where a gas station defined the edge of the settlement.

A bus came along before long and, donning her wimple, she wheedled a grudging ride to Acuna from the driver as an act of Christian charity. The bus ride took nearly three grueling hours. The urine smell of the conveyance was on the verge of overcoming her when the driver announced her destination sourly. She made her way past a dozen tired-looking laborers and various old women, runny-nosed children, chickens, suitcases and shopping bags of produce to the exit. The gaudily painted bus pulled away in a cloud of dust, and she looked around at Acuna. If the last village had been small, this one was minuscule.

A half-dozen houses crouched around a single business that looked to be part grocery, part gas station, part post office, part who-knew-what-else. Warily, she headed for it. A dull-eyed man greeted her when she ducked into the low-ceilinged room.

"Do you have a telephone I could use?" she asked.

"You pay for the call."

"I will when I get off the phone." She hoped. If she was lucky, Father Ambrose would figure out a way to wire her money and maybe a replacement credit card in this god-forsaken bit of nowhere.

"No way. Pay first."

Drat. Change of tactics. She asked, "Can you tell me where Ms. Ferrosa lives?"

The man laughed. "*Grandma* Ferrosa lives in the last house on the right, that way."

"Perfect. I don't need to use your phone, then." She stepped outside into a morning that was rapidly heating up toward a miserably hot afternoon.

The Ferrosa house wasn't much to look at on the outside. But the inside was neat and surprisingly roomy, with one large, central room taking up most of the space. An incredibly wrinkled woman answered the door. The top of her head came up maybe to Elise's chin.

No sign of two small children in the house. She took a deep breath and plunged in, hoping against hope she was at the right place. "Hello. I am Sister Mary Elise. I'm here to take the children to safety."

"The Lord has answered my prayers and sent His messenger!" the elderly woman exclaimed.

Elise winced. She was a lot of things, but God's messenger was not one of them. But in short order, she was hustled inside, parked at a rough wooden table, and a heaping plate of black beans and rice plunked down before her.

"Are the children here?" she asked around a mouthful of the delicious concoction that turned out to be laced with spicy sausage and cooked into a smoky stew.

"Visiting my niece and her children today. They will be back for supper."

Elise asked, "You don't happen to have a telephone, do you?"

"I do." The woman reached into the pocket of her apron and pulled out a shockingly high-tech cell phone, which she passed to Elise.

Gratefully, she dialed the United States country code followed by Father Ambrose's phone number. She nearly sobbed in relief at the sound of his voice saying hello.

"It's me, Elise. I think I've found the kids. But I'm in a bit of trouble and need your help."

"Where are you?"

"I'm in Acuna."

"Are the children all right?"

"I haven't seen them yet, but I'm told they're fine. That's not the problem. I've lost all my money and documentation."

"How did you manage that, child?"

"Long story short: we were ambushed by rebels, who were attacked by soldiers. In fleeing the scene, my pouch with all my personal things and medical supplies got left behind."

"We?"

"An even longer story." And one she didn't plan to tell just now. "I need you to wire me a little expense money and see about replacing my passport or getting me some sort of paperwork so I can get on a plane for the States."

Travel waivers for the Garza children had already been arranged through the Apostolic Nunciature of the Holy See in Bogota, which was a fancy title for the Vatican Embassy to Colombia. But she was out of luck. Worst case, she could put the kids on a plane by themselves and follow them home later. But they were awfully small to travel alone. A motherly instinct she didn't even know she had reared up in protest at the idea. Where had *that* come from?

Father Ambrose interrupted her unpleasant train of

thought. "I'll see what I can do. It may take me a day or two. Will you be all right until then?"

"I think so. But hurry." The last thing she needed was for Drago to come after her and find her still in Acuna. As attractive as he might be, she and the children were better off *not* in the company of a violent criminal being hunted by the government, as surely he would be after last night's shoot-out.

"The woman currently watching after the kids can probably be convinced to put me up for that long. She seems the friendly type."

"Need me to talk to her?"

"It wouldn't hurt." Elise passed the phone to the elderly woman, who took it, frowning in confusion. As the woman listened, her face cleared and even took on a reverent expression. The woman smiled and nodded at her, and Elise's alarm grew. What was the padre saying to put that awed expression on the poor woman's face?

Grandma disconnected the call. "It is a great honor to help you. A great honor, indeed. May God bless you and your work, Sister."

What on earth did he say about her? Not that she was about to look this gift horse in the mouth. Abashed, she managed not to roll her eyes as the woman took her hand and kissed it.

"You will stay here until everything is arranged," Grandma ordered.

Elise nodded. "But only if you let me help you with the cooking and cleaning."

Grandma protested, but Elise stood her ground. She wasn't a freeloader and never had been. She'd pull her weight around here and that was that. As the afternoon progressed, it became clear that the older woman thought she was some sort of saint in the making. The woman kept mumbling prayers to her and kissing her hand at every opportunity. It was tough to stomach. Elise felt like the worst kind of fraud by the time dinner was served and a pack of six children came tumbling loudly into the house.

Oh, God. They had the look of their father about them. There was no question in Elise's mind which two were Mia and Emanuel. They had the same aristocratic features and dark-lashed, golden-hazel eyes as their father. She'd stared at Valdiron's picture for so long, she even noticed the nuance of his ears in the children, the way his throat turned into small shoulders shaped like his. Oh, yes. They were Garzas, through and through.

The eldest, six-year-old Mia, was shy and hung on to Grandma's skirts when they were introduced. When bright-eyed Emanuel would have bounded over her to say hello, his older sister grabbed him by the arm and pulled him back. Cautious child, she was. Elise noted with a pang that the little girl's eyes looked far too old for her years.

She'd worked in enough emergency rooms to recognize a traumatized child and to know not to rush her. She merely smiled pleasantly at the little girl and included her in the chatter of the other children over supper, but made no special effort to approach Mia.

After the meal, the children ran outside to play in the backyard, and Elise kept an eye on the children through the kitchen window as she washed and dried the dishes. Mia promised to grow into a great beauty—but then, Valdiron had always had a penchant for fashion models and had been a handsome man himself. The face of an angel, the soul of a demon.

Elise watched carefully for any signs of violence or aggression in the children's play, and beyond Emanuel snatching a truck out of two-year-old Guillermo's hands, she saw nothing to indicate the children had inherited their father's psychopathic tendencies. Emanuel reminded her of a rambunctious puppy. He ran and tumbled and tussled nonstop with the other children and collapsed, exhausted, when bedtime came. Whatever darkness had touched Mia's life appeared not to have touched him at all.

When Grandma had tucked in all the children and the house grew quiet once more, Elise poured hot water into a pair of white china cups she found on a shelf and made tea for herself and the older woman.

Grandma fell into a chair heavily. "It is hard keeping up with so many bambinos. I am too old for it."

"You're doing a wonderful job with them. They're happy and healthy." They were a lot luckier than many children in this war-torn region. "Tell me. Do you know what has put that haunted look in Mia's eyes?"

"Aah, you are as wise as that priest on the phone said you are."

Wise? He'd called her wise? Hah! Liar.

"Mia was with her father when he died. From what little she's told me, I gather he was shot many times. But he did not die right away. She has nightmares of trying to stop the bleeding."

Elise's heart twisted. She realized with a start that, at some subconscious level, she'd wished for Garza's offspring to suffer. But not like this. Not a little girl lost among strangers and trying so hard to be grown up and brave. To look out for her baby brother.

And then it hit her. This was why Father Ambrose had sent her down here on this particular mission. He'd wanted her to see the human side of her quest for vengeance. This little girl's suffering was the direct result of her efforts to bring Garza to justice.

She'd been one of the foremost investigators of his activities and had been pivotal in exposing his criminal activities to the world press. She'd set the Colombian Truth Commission upon these children's father, and they'd been the ones to gun him down. At the end of the day, *she* was responsible for the haunted look in that child's eyes.

A sob escaped her.

Grandma was beside her immediately, taking her ice cold hands in warm, paper-dry ones. "Do not be sad, Sister. You will take them to a new life. A happy place where they can grow up safe and free. They will never know suffering or fear again. You will see to it."

And so she would. She owed it to Mia and Emanuel Garza. Heck, she owed them her life if it came to it.

Damn Father Ambrose to hell and back. He'd known exactly what he was doing to her when he sent her down here. He couldn't have thought up a more diabolical penance for her transgressions if he'd tried. He'd said all along that revenge only hurt the person seeking it. And oh, how right he was.

While Grandma patted her hand, offering consolation she didn't deserve, Elise broke down and cried for the second time in as many days. She cried for her own dead parents, for all the years she'd wasted in anger and hate, for all the pain she'd caused these innocent children. She cursed their father for putting them in harm's way by bringing them into the world at all, but then she recanted the curse. She couldn't fault even a monster for wanting to create something good and pure.

And now their care and protection had fallen to her. No power on earth was going to harm those two children while she lived and breathed. That she vowed solemnly before God.

No doubt Father Ambrose had known full well she'd do that, too, once she looked Mia and Emanuel in the eyes. He'd trapped her as neatly as a rabbit in a snare.

# *Chapter 7*

He was going to kill Elise. Flat out. When he found her—and he would—he was going to wring her neck.

Ted fumed as the bartender mumbled through a bunch of lame excuses about how the nun must have slipped out through the bathroom window and disappeared. The only saving grace was he knew exactly where she was headed. To Acuna. To get those kids. Reluctant admiration for her sheer cussedness passed through him. They were two lucky children to have her on their side.

Now all he had to do was break away from Raoul and his top lieutenants for long enough to go find Elise and drag her happy self back here where he could keep an eye on her and protect her from her own naiveté. Assuming she didn't get herself killed, or worse, before he could get to her.

His attention snapped back sharply to Raoul, though, when the man commented a shade too casually, "You do not look like I expected."

Crapcrapcrapcrapcrap. This was what they'd all feared at H.O.T. Watch Ops. That Ted would bump into someone who'd actually met the real Drago Cantori and would identify him as an imposter. He counted fast. Nine men, all armed, all alert and with hands near their weapons. He couldn't drop them all. But if he could take out Raoul and those two guys over by the door, he might just make it out of here alive—

Even he knew when he was hopelessly outnumbered. He had to *talk* his way out of this pickle, if for no other reason than because Elise needed him. With desperate calm, he said to Raoul, "A man in my line of work has to be careful. I make a point of people thinking I look differently than I do." He leaned forward and lowered his voice to a conspiratorial murmur. "I'll let you in on a little secret. I hire actors to impersonate me from time to time. It helps spread confusion about what I really look like."

Raoul nodded thoughtfully. "A clever idea."

"It's expensive, but I've found it to be worth the cost over the years." He took a sip of his coffee and added casually, "I even had my sister impersonate me once."

Raoul laughed. "Did she cost you money on that deal?"

Ted snorted. "You wouldn't ask that if you'd met her. She knows more about weapons than anyone I've ever met, and she's a far sight meaner than me."

Raoul's grin widened. "What's she up to now?"

"She's in jail. She killed some Americans in a nightclub bombing and the Feds caught up with her."

The look in Raoul's eyes was far too knowing. The bastard already knew exactly what had happened to Annika Cantori. That had been a test. Ted swore silently. Had he passed?

Raoul spit on the floor. "Bah. American *federales*."

The Army of Freedom man turned away and called

for coffee. When steaming mugs of black liquid were set before them, Ted lifted his in a silent toast. Crud. His hand was shaking. He lowered the drink quickly.

His companion relaxed and commenced joking about do-gooder nuns who ran around the jungle. Although the subject made him much more tense than he dared let on, at least it appeared that he'd successfully navigated the minefield of Raoul's questions about his Drago Cantori identity. But it had been a damned close call. The way Enrique had explained it, Raoul was the big kahuna in this Army of Freedom outfit. If he wasn't a hundred percent sure what the real Drago Cantori looked like, odds were no one else in the organization was, either.

Now that he'd passed this particular gauntlet, his fake identity should hold up going forward. Ted let out a careful breath.

Raoul was speaking again. "…tell me. What are the odds you can obtain more…powerful…weapons than just small arms?"

Ted took another sip of coffee before answering. This was exactly why he'd been sent out on this mission. To find out what the real Drago Cantori had been up to before he'd been killed in the Cayman Islands. Ted considered his companion. If he appeared too eager to talk to Raoul, the man would become even more suspicious than he already was. Respond too cautiously, and Raoul would find himself another arms dealer.

Finally, Ted replied, "Depends on how much more powerful we're talking. What did you have in mind?"

"Something impressive."

Ted leaned back in his chair and smile expansively. "I can do impressive. Do you prefer a particular flavor of impressive?"

Raoul frowned, hesitating. Wow. He must be contemplating something serious if it gave even him pause to say it aloud.

Ted helped the guy out, prompting, "Tell me this. What is your target? Soldiers? Civilians? A building? A city? Are you after maximum damage or maximum casualties?"

The insurgent seemed to relax as Ted talked calmly of weapons of mass destruction as if they were a realistic possibility.

"An airplane. Maximum casualties."

Ted nodded slowly, fighting like crazy to hide his shock. Maximum casualties meant an airliner full of civilians. Since when were Colombian freedom fighters in the business of blowing up passenger jets? That was the traditional purview of straight terrorists.

The hot, strong coffee suddenly tasted bitter in his mouth. He answered evenly, "It takes a missile to shoot down an airplane. They're expensive and relatively difficult to obtain. Frankly, a daisy chain of small explosions in a populated place would kill as many or more people as knocking a jet out of the sky. And it would cause a hell of a lot more immediate chaos. Not to mention the explosives for something like that are cheap and easy to get. Keep in mind that using a surface-to-air missile properly takes training. It also takes tight internal discipline for an organization to pull off something like shooting down an airplane."

Raoul grimaced, which spoke volumes about what he thought of his own organization's internal discipline. Duly noted.

Ted leaned forward and lowered his voice. "Don't get me wrong. I can get you a missile, no problem. I'm just suggesting a cheaper and easier alternative, too." Grinning, he added, "Let it never be said I'm not an ethical guy."

The rebel leader laughed heartily at the irony, breaking the tension of the moment as Ted had intended for it to do.

Raoul answered without hesitation, "I want the missile. Several of them, in fact. Can you deliver?"

Several? This guy was planning something on the scale of 9/11 then? Stunned, his thoughts slid to the next logical question. Who was the target? Would the man go after a single airport, or maybe many airports scattered across a nation or several nations? Would it be a simultaneous attack for maximum shock value, or several individual attacks spread out over time so as not to look related to one another?

Ted hid his dismay carefully. This was exactly why he was here. To answer those sorts of questions. His thoughts churned on. If Raoul aimed his attack at airports in places like Caracas and Bogota, the people of Colombia who supported the Army of Freedom would turn on them in fury. The rebels would lose all support. Unless—his thoughts derailed sharply—unless the target was not in Colombia.

Was this guy looking to become a player on the international stage? But surely Raoul knew the international response would be fierce and fast. Was the rebel counting on that to rally support from within Colombia? Maybe use the inevitable retaliation from the attacked country to topple the Colombian regime? Unite the various insurgent groups against a common external foe?

Who was the target? As if it took a rocket scientist to deduce *that* answer. Who better to cast as the invading villain than the United States? South Americans already resented the perceived high-handedness with which America had dealt with them in the past. The Colombian government had spent years shouting about how American oil companies were trying to rip off the Colombian people for the country's petroleum reserves. Hating America would be an easy sell to many Colombians, particularly to those mired in poverty and frustration.

He could see it now. This guy would shoot down a bunch of American airplanes, the U.S. would figure out who did it, they'd come down to Colombia to take out the Army of Freedom, and the Colombian people would see it as an attack of a larger bully upon a small, poor, local group of freedom fighters. It was a decent plan, actually. Worse, it stood a chance of working.

Ted set down his coffee cup. "Surface-to-air missiles are definitely obtainable. They are expensive, though, and must be moved discreetly. I have the resources to do that. The question is, do you?"

"I have a few men with the training to use such a weapon."

Good grief. Raoul had a unit of former military men working for him? Mercenaries, maybe? But very few mercenaries would participate in the kind of mass attack this man was planning. No money was worth the manhunt to follow. Raoul's special team had to be zealots, then. Men like Valdiron Garza and his cadre, who'd believed that the ends justified any means, including the most extreme violence.

The beginnings of a headache throbbed behind Ted's eyes. God, he was tired of these games. Of men like this. Would they never stop coming? It seemed as though for every one he killed, two more came to take the dead one's place. "Tell me something, Raoul. What do you believe in?"

"Pardon?"

Ted made eye contact with the would-be terrorist. "What do you believe in so strongly that you're willing to use such a weapon? I can't just hand these things out to anybody who wants one, you understand. You need to have a cause."

"You presume to judge the worthiness of my cause?" Raoul half stood, his voice rising in insult.

Ted answered blandly, "Not at all. I presume to test how serious you are about going through with such a deal. These types of weapons are tracked carefully, and I will have to lie low for some time after I do this deal. I need to be absolutely certain you won't back out of the deal and leave me holding an expensive—and very hot—cache of weapons I haven't gotten paid for."

Raoul sank back into his chair. "Aah. I see your thinking. You worry only about profit, while I worry about the creeping spread of American influence on this continent."

Bingo. His guess about the target had been correct. He tuned out the usual anti-American spiel that Raoul devolved into. At the end of it, he shrugged and said only, "I am a merchant, not a philosopher."

"I think we understand one another, Drago."

"I'll make a few calls."

Ted excused himself and stepped outside. He dialed a phone number that hooked into his operational headquarters and murmured quietly, "You get all that?"

"Roger, sir. Commander Hathaway says to make the deal. We can come up with a few deactivated missiles to deliver."

"Will do. Oh, and can you tell me how far I am from a village called Acuna?"

"One moment." The phone went silent. "It's about eighty kilometers northwest of your position. A bus runs from your current location through there every morning."

That would explain how Elise just disappeared out from under everyone's noses. Clever girl.

"Anything we should be aware of in Acuna, sir?"

"Nope. Just asking. Thanks."

He disconnected the call. First the nun. Then the missiles.

Getting away from Raoul was a piece of cake. Ted rolled underneath his Jeep, fetched the magnetic key box he'd secreted earlier on the underside of the chassis, and used the spare key to start the engine. When a low-level flunky tried to detain him, he told the guy he was leaving to arrange Raoul's arms deal for him. The guy shrugged and let him go.

Finding Acuna wasn't all that hard, either. It wasn't as if there were a million roads out here. He took the only one that led northwest out of the village, confident that it would eventually run into Acuna. He'd been driving about an hour when he came to a small settlement. A quick word with a local confirmed that this road would, indeed take him to his destination. It was apparently about thirty klicks on down the road. However, the man seemed alarmed when he heard the name Acuna. That gave Ted pause.

"Is there some danger in Acuna I should know of, amigo?" he asked the farmer.

The Colombian shrugged. "People hear things. Rumors."

His alarm deepened. Elise was in Acuna. "And what do the rumors say of Acuna?"

"This and that." The man's dark-skinned face gave away absolutely nothing. Ted had seen the stony expression a thousand times. Locals all over the world had the same natural suspicion of outsiders, no matter how much that outsider could help their plight.

Reluctant to talk, huh? Ted reached for his wallet, but the farmer waved him off before the leather cleared his back pocket. Crap. The reason the guy wasn't talking was fear, then. Not good.

He said quietly, "Look. I'm going to Acuna because I

have a friend there. A nun. She gives the locals medical care. I'm supposed to pick her up and move her to another village today."

"A nun?" The man abruptly looked distressed. "Then you'd better hurry, *paisano*. The Colombian Army's headed that way."

The army? What did that bunch want with an out-of-the-way little hole-in-the-wall like Acuna? Did it have something to do with Elise or the kids she was supposed to rescue?

He asked carefully, "Is there any group in that area that might...object...to the army's presence?"

The man nodded vigorously, but aloud merely said, "I know nothing. I say nothing. I no get in trouble."

Curses erupted unbidden in his brain. *Not good.* Elise and her kids were in that village, and it was about to become a combat zone. An urgent need to save them made his entire body buzz with tension. Ted grasped the man's shoulder briefly. "Thank you. I'll get that nun out of there as fast as I can."

"And then go west. Even a lion will not charge into a nest of vipers."

Which was a euphemistic way of the guy saying that no Colombian Army patrol would barge into the bulk of the Army of Freedom, which apparently was west of Acuna. Also good to know. "I understand, *señor*. Thanks again. God bless you."

The man nodded soberly. "Save the sister."

The wisdom of Elise masquerading as a nun was more apparent than ever. That farmer hadn't been willing to say a thing until he heard that a person of the cloth was in danger. Then he'd spilled his guts.

In a state shockingly close to panic, Ted drove as fast as the Jeep could go over the rutted road without ripping out its transmission. He slowed only as the jungle gave way to patches of farmed land, announcing an upcoming village. If the farmer had been accurate, this would be Acuna.

A faint, deep noise caught his attention. Dismayed, he stopped the vehicle to listen more closely. He rolled down the window but heard nothing. He cut the engine, and silence fell around him. There it was again. A low, ominous rumble that he—veteran of years of military action—recognized immediately. His blood ran cold. Acuna was under attack.

Adrenaline jangling through him so hard he could barely dial his satellite phone, he called H.O.T. Watch headquarters on the crisis line reserved for operators in trouble. It overrode all the normal phone lines into the surveillance facility.

"Go," a voice bit out on the other end of the line.

"I'm approaching Acuna, Colombia. I've got mortar fire and need immediate satellite recon."

"Say mission," the controller on the other end replied tersely.

He thought fast. Part of special operators' job around the world was to guard the safety of Americans abroad. It would do as an excuse to justify using H.O.T. Watch's formidable resources to save Elise. "Civilian rescue. An American woman and two children."

"Roger. Telemetry is coming up now. Say your status."

"Not yet engaged. The players are unaware of my presence."

"Roger."

A new voice came up on the line. He recognized his boss, Navy Commander Brady Hathaway. "What's up, Drago?"

They'd decided to use his assumed name as his call

sign on this mission. "I need to get into Acuna. There's a woman—"

His boss interrupted sharply. "And she pertains to your mission how?"

Ted sighed. He knew the drill. Soldiers were emphatically not supposed to get involved with civilians on missions. Particularly female ones. But he needed H.O.T. Watch's help if was going to get into the village and get out with Elise in the midst of a massive firefight between the Colombian Army and the Army of Freedom. He replied, "She's a nun, sir. An American."

Hathaway swore under his breath, something to the effect of do-gooders barging in where angels fear to tread.

"You have *no* idea," Ted retorted. "This one has a freaking death wish."

"Will this rescue interfere with your primary mission?" Hathaway asked perceptively.

It already had. He'd snuck out of Raoul's camp, potentially pissing off the rebel mightily. For all he knew, he might have already blown the mission. "The nun seems to get a free pass into the rebel camps. She's a nurse and a hell of a cook. She won't hurt my mission." Although, not kissing her again, and soon, might just kill him.

Another series of low booms echoed across the valley.

Hathaway reported briskly, "Colombian Army forces are firing on what appears to be a rebel patrol pinned down approximately two hundred meters northeast of Acuna. Do you have reason to believe sympathizers with the Army of Freedom are located in the village?"

"Without a doubt, sir."

"That explains the attack, then. Okay, enhanced telemetry's coming up on screen. Acuna consists of eight structures. One appears to be a business. Probably a general store. There's a gas pump out front. The remainder are dwellings. We show no movement in the village at this time. Unconfirmed assessment: the locals are hiding or have fled."

"Best approach?"

"Jungle comes within thirty meters of the east side of the village. But that brings you close to the rebel position. You will likely draw their fire if they spot you."

Grim determination to protect Elise and her charges flowed through him. "Then I guess they'd better not spot me."

"You going in wired for sound?"

"Hell, yes." He was no idiot. He wasn't too proud to use the full resources of H.O.T. Watch Ops to stay alive. To that end, he moved around to the back of the Jeep and was relieved to see that Raoul's boys hadn't removed his large duffel bag of military gear from the vehicle's cargo area. He spotted Elise's medical bag, too. If only he got a chance to return it to her.

He donned a Kevlar vest, throat microphone and utility belt with a full compliment of ammunition, grenades and miscellaneous gear. He smeared camo paint on his face fast and jammed a floppy hat on his head to break up his profile. He plucked some weeds and stuck them in his belt and the brim of his hat. Lastly, he slung an MP-7 over his shoulder. The small, semi-automatic weapon was ideal for short-range combat in heavy cover like a jungle or urban setting.

"Moving out," he announced grimly.

Elise ducked as a loud explosion sounded nearby. Mia screamed and ran for Grandma, who hugged the little girl close and began reciting a Hail Mary. "What was that?" Elise cried.

Grandma interrupted her Hail Mary long enough to grunt, "Army."

What were *they* doing here? Did they know about Garza's children? Were they here to snatch the kids or kill them? Was this what it had been like for her parents the day Garza and his men had come for them? Panic threatened to overwhelm her. "We have to leave," she told Grandma tersely.

"We must pray to Heavenly Father and the Blessed Virgin," Grandma groaned as another explosion rocked the house.

Somehow, Elise didn't think prayer was going to save them from this attack. She replied urgently, "God expects people of faith to take action to save themselves. We've got to get out of here. *Now.*" If she'd been there, she'd have told her parents the exact same thing. Would they have listened to her? Could she have saved them if she'd only been there? She *had* to save the children in her care, now.

Emanuel ran in just then and headed straight for Elise. He wrapped his arms around her legs so tightly she couldn't even walk properly. She bent down and peeled him off her thigh, lifting him into her arms. "Come on, Grandma. This way."

The older woman stopped long enough to grab a black shawl and a small, lumpy bag while Elise moved into the doorway to assess the situation outside. Sounds of gunfire erupted somewhere behind them. It sounded as though the fighting was on the east side of town. They would head west, then. There was a fair bit of open farmland in that direction, but if they stuck to the hedgerows separating the fields and went slow, they should have enough cover… she hoped.

Grandma led Mia by the hand while Elise shifted Emanuel to piggybacking on her back. He cried against her neck, squealing every time a loud explosion blasted behind them. She didn't shush him. Over the noise of the fighting, she doubted anyone would hear one little boy's terror.

They cleared the village quickly and began the careful trek across the fields. She just prayed none of them stepped on any deadly snakes as they waded through the tall grass and brush at the edge of the nearest field. Grandma and Mia went first, setting a pace the elderly woman could maintain.

Shouting erupted behind them, and Elise dropped to the ground. Emanuel slid off her back, cowering against her side. She turned to look back at the village and was appalled to see soldiers breaking down doors and barging inside each house. Automatic weapon fire erupted inside one. Had her parents listened to their friends and neighbors being gunned down like this? She closed her eyes briefly and said a quick prayer for the souls of the unfortunate inhabitants who'd disastrously decided to hide rather than flee. Had her parents prayed together for salvation? Knowing them they had.

The older woman crossed herself, and Elise belatedly—angrily—mimicked the motion. God didn't save anyone. People saved themselves. "We've got to keep moving," she snapped at Grandma.

This time, she held Emanuel's hand as the four of them crept forward. The boy's eyes were huge with fright. Her unreasoning anger at her parents drained away, leaving behind only grief.

"Emanuel," she whispered. "Pretend we're spies with important information that will defeat the bad guys and win the war for the good guys. We're sneaking back to our own camp to share our news and will be great heroes."

The child nodded. It took a minute or two, but the terror

on his face eased slightly as he escaped into the game. If only she could do the same. But she was all too aware of the danger they faced. She'd seen the results of civilians caught in the cross fire. She'd heard the screams, seen the wounds and mutilation, the vacant stares and tearing grief. Heck, she recalled all too well being that person, herself.

She would never forget the day her family had been the targets. She'd left her parents in a village while she went on a day hike with some local youths to picnic and see a waterfall.

The government officially supported missionaries and their work. But unofficially, elements within the regime— namely Valdiron Garza—had been convinced that missionaries stirred up the peasants against the government. He'd blamed the missionaries for the violence sweeping across the country. It wasn't true, but that didn't matter. A scapegoat had to be found, and who better than a bunch of foreigners who wouldn't take violent action to defend themselves.

When she and the others had returned from the outing, she'd smelled it first. A metallic scent of blood had floated out of the village on a gentle breeze. And then the unnatural silence had registered. Garza's men had slaughtered every living creature in the town, down to the last chicken. She and the others had run for the village. Screams and moans from the others had started before she got to the farmhouse at which she and her parents had been staying.

The house had been empty. She'd been hopeful at first that they'd escaped. Silly her. There had been blood, though. She'd followed the trail of it out the back door and into the low shed that served as a barn. And that had been when she'd spotted them. They'd been strung up from the rafters by their wrists like animals for the slaughter and were barely recognizable as human.

Elise stumbled as the agony of that memory rolled over her. Even now, nearly six years later, it had the power to destroy her. A small hand tightened in hers, startling her. She glanced down and caught Emanuel's huge, frightened gaze. They were the same, the two of them. Orphans both. Victims of violence beyond their control. Traumatized and terrified.

She squeezed his hand reassuringly.

"Remember, we're superspies," he whispered.

Her heart broke a little, but she managed to smile back, "You're right." She glanced ahead at Mia. Did the little girl carry memories as horrifying as hers? Did she have the same bloody nightmares? The same pervasive terror that she was next? The same sense of helplessness and hopelessness? She wouldn't wish her experience on her worst enemy, let alone a six-year-old child.

It took maybe twenty minutes to creep and crawl into the first underbrush west of town, but it felt like hours. Days. Finally, though, a canopy of green closed in overhead. The sporadic sounds of the battle behind them dulled, muffled by the jungle's humid embrace.

She'd fled into the jungle that day, too. Thankfully, some of the others had kept their heads better than her. They'd guided her to another village a few kilometers away. Put her on a bus and told her to go home.

She'd refused at first. She had to get their bodies. Give them a proper burial. The others had pointed to the pillar of smoke and sparks rising over the ridge behind them as darkness fell. The army had seen to removing all evidence of the massacre. There would be no bodies left to bury.

"Look," Mia whispered urgently.

Elise glanced back to where the child pointed and, through a small gap in the trees, saw black smoke billowing up into the sky. She groaned aloud. It was too much.

Too close to history repeating itself. Her knees collapsed and she sank into the wet leaves.

Grandma bent down to pat her shoulder and murmured implacably, "It was just a house. Just things. We are alive because of your quick action. And that is what matters."

Someone had said something similar to her that day, too. Lucky for them they'd gone on the hike or they'd be dead, too. It hadn't comforted her then, and it didn't now.

"I'm so sorry," she gasped.

Grandma frowned. "For what? You did nothing but save us."

"I got you into this—"

"No, you didn't. I knew exactly who those children were when I agreed to take them in. My daughter was a maid in their home and she told me they were sweet babies who'd never done anything to anyone."

The admission startled Elise. "Why did you do it, then? Particularly if you knew who they were and that something like this could happen?"

The older woman's voice was deep and wise. "Now, Sister, you know how it is when you listen to your heart. Mine told me it was the right thing to do. So I took them in and got on with it. God will take care of the rest."

The woman's indomitable faith was humbling. Elise knew without a shadow of a doubt she had no such strength within her. "Speaking of which, is there another village nearby? Do you know anyone in the area with whom we can stay?"

Grandma nodded. "There's a village about ten kilometers west of here. We might reach it by nightfall."

Elise was alarmed. Over six miles? Grandma was no spring chicken. Her back was hunched and her legs bowed with age. "Can you make it that far?" she asked doubtfully.

"The Lord will give me strength." Her eyes twinkled as she added, "And I'm not quite dead, yet."

Elise had forgotten how tough the people were in this part of the world. Life had to be wrestled from the land by sheer force of will. She struck out in the direction Grandma indicated. The going was miserable at first, but then they found a footpath heading in the general direction they wanted. It probably was made and used by drug runners or rebels, and she trod it gingerly. She really didn't need to run into any violent insurgents with an elderly woman and two small children in tow.

True to her word, Grandma held up for the long hike. They actually had to stop more often for the children to rest than for her. Mia was silent and uncomplaining, but Elise didn't like the haunted look in her eyes. The child was far too aware of the fate they'd just escaped and appeared to be reliving nightmares of her own.

She gathered Mia's stiff body in her lap, hugging the child in spite of her apparent resistance to being comforted. She'd been Mia herself. She knew exactly how badly the child needed reassurance. She might not deserve love herself, but this child certainly did. "Sweetie," she whispered, "I'll never let anyone hurt you. I promise. And I'll keep promising that until you believe me."

She thought she felt the little girl relax fractionally.

"You're the bravest little girl I've ever met. Not much longer, and then you won't have to be brave anymore. You and me, we'll have a little cry together, and then we'll both feel better."

Elise's heart melted as the child's thin arms squeezed her neck in the briefest of hugs. It was a start. By golly, she'd help Mia make the long climb back to happiness if it killed her. Although she sincerely hoped it didn't come to that. She rather liked being alive.

It turned out Grandma's lumpy bag was a few handy survival supplies, including a knife, a collapsible jug, and to Elise's delicate American gut's vast relief, a tiny brown bottle of water purification tablets. During one of their breaks by a stream, while they waited for the water she'd scooped into the jug to become safe to drink, Elise sat down beside Mia again.

"How are you doing, short stuff?"

The little girl merely shrugged. Elise winced. God, how she knew the feeling of being unable to express the horror consuming her.

"I was pretty scared at first when we left the village," Elise commented, "but then I remembered that God looks out especially for children. And since I'm with you and your brother, I figure I'll be safe, too."

"You think?" Mia mumbled.

"I know. Have you ever heard stories about how fiercely a mother jaguar protects her cubs?"

Mia nodded.

"Well, jaguars are wimps compared to human mommies. And the way I see it, you and Emanuel are my cubs now. I bet if you asked Grandma, she'd say the same thing. God sent you not one but two fierce mama jaguars to look out for you. He must think you and your brother are pretty special. Grandma and I, we'll do whatever it takes to keep the two of you safe."

"You can't be a mother. You're a nun."

"Ha. Try me. I'm a jaguar." She growled and tickled the little girl until she giggled. Elise pulled Mia into her lap and gave her another big hug. She was going to keep on hugging and tickling and talking to Mia until that giggle came to her as easily as breathing.

The child drew in a wobbly breath and released it slowly. Aah, what Elise wouldn't have given to have somebody take her in their lap and hold her close after her parents had died. It hadn't been until Father Ambrose climbed up on that bridge beside her that she'd felt any connection to any other human being at all. He'd been her first and only reminder for a long time that human beings were capable of as much kindness and compassion as they were of cruelty.

Thank God her path had led her to this little girl within a few weeks of Garza's death. Now, if only she could share enough love and compassion to reach past Mia's grief and mistrust of mankind in the same way Father Ambrose had for her. She cursed the priest good-naturedly in her head. He was a sly one, he was, to send her to these children with whom she had so very much in common.

"Are we ready to head out again?" Elise asked more cheerfully than she felt. "The superhero league is waiting for our report, fellow superspies."

Emanuel, recharged after a few minutes of rest, bounded to his feet. "Let's go!"

Elise made everyone take a big drink of water and re-filled the jug before they waded across the stream. Her legs hurt and her back was tired. But if Grandma could do this without a whimper, then so could she. As they headed out, the older woman's gaze caught hers, and her rheumy eyes twinkled. Grandma knew full well she was shaming all of them into not complaining. She was a tough old bird, all right. Elise grinned back. They continued on, ever deeper into the jungle.

Ted ducked into the shadow of a palmetto bush and swore under his breath. Helpless rage tore through him as army soldiers streamed into the village, breaking down doors and shooting anything that moved. He couldn't begin to stop them all. If Elise and the kids were still in Acuna, he was about to witness their grisly deaths.

He had to *do* something. Had to save them!

He muttered urgently, "I need infrared imaging ASAP. Any children inside any of these buildings?" He figured wherever the kids were, that would be where Elise was.

"Negative. Five adults in the fifth building on your left, but that's it."

Automatic weapon fire erupted from that very building just then. Make that five dead adults. Normally, he watched this sort of slaughter with cold detachment. It wasn't that he was unaffected by death, particularly the death of innocents. But he had a job to do. And that required him maintaining the ability to think coolly and rationally in the face of violence. He'd feel bad about the dead people later.

For just a moment, he wondered how many orphans he'd created over the years. How many parents had he killed in the line of duty? He shoved the thought aside. He'd just been doing his job. That was all that mattered, right?

For a moment there, however, when he'd thought Elise might be gunned down before him, he'd nearly panicked. Only a decade's worth of discipline, pounded into him by a hundred encounters like this one, saved him from doing something suicidally stupid. He was definitely losing the touch for this sort of stuff. A low-level hum of dismay started low in his gut. What was he supposed to do when he could no longer do this? *Later.* He'd think about that later. Right now he had an intensely irritating nun and her charges to track down.

His relief that Elise and the kids had apparently made it out of Acuna made him light-headed. He took a deep, steadying breath. She was okay. The kids were okay.

Except he'd never even met her blasted orphans. Why was he so concerned about them, anyway? The answer came to him but tasted sour on his tongue. He cared about them because Elise cared about them. What was important to her was apparently important to him. *And when had that unpleasant little development taken place?*

Scowling, he snapped into his microphone, "Any idea where the inhabitants of the village have gone?"

"We picked up telemetry of some folks making their way west into the jungle. They're probably hiding until the army and the rebels clear out."

Abject relief flowed through him. It had to have been Elise. She'd gotten the children out to safety. Thank God. That being the case, his work here was done. He had no need to get into the middle of a firefight that didn't involve him or his mission. "Roger, H.O.T. Watch. I'm out of here."

"Be advised, it looks like your friend, Raoul, has just arrived. The tracking burr you put on him is working perfectly," the H.O.T. Watch controller surprised him by announcing.

He swore under his breath. "Is he alone?" Ted bit out.

"Nope. He and three Jeep-loads of guys just rolled up on the rebel position."

"Is that enough to take the army patrol?"

"Not with the army's armaments. If the army figures out a major rebel leader is in range, they'll hit Raoul and company with everything they've got."

He thought back to the mortar- and shoulder-launched-rocket fire he'd been hearing. Surprised, he asked, "You mean the army hasn't used everything they've got, yet?"

"Not even close. They've got close to fifty men, rocket-propelled grenade launchers and heavy artillery. They'll shred the jungle and everyone in it if they cut loose."

Killing Raoul would neatly solve his immediate problem of stopping the Army of Freedom from blowing up a bunch of civilian airliners. Except for the fact that some new leader would step into the power vacuum caused by Raoul's death. Which would leave him back at square zero in making contact with the Army of Freedom leadership. And who knew what grandiose schemes the next leader would cook up in the meantime? Like it or not, he had to go save Raoul.

His gut pulled him west, toward Elise and the children. But his head told him he had to stay here. See this battle through for the sake of his primary mission. He had to get word to the rebels to bug out and not take on this army force today.

Ted sighed. "How far south do I have to go to circle around behind the Army of Freedom position so I can approach them from the rear?"

"Four hundred meters should do it."

"Roger. Moving out." He couldn't believe he was about to save a bunch of rebel insurgents from the legitimate government of this country. But that was the nature of his work. Covert ops made for strange bedfellows. An image of Elise in his bed flashed through his head. He shoved aside the image hastily. Not going to happen. Ever. *Get over it. Get over her.* For some reason, however, his psyche wasn't on board with that concept. Face it, he lectured himself as he crawled through the underbrush. She was hot and he wanted her, wimple or no.

His boss's voice came up on his earbud. "You sure about bailing these guys out? You're walking into a potential cluster storm."

"This whole damned mission is a cluster storm," he muttered back as he crawled on his belly into the towering wall of jungle.

# Chapter 8

Elise would've seriously considered sobbing in relief as the jungle opened up and a small town came into sight were it not for the kids and the fact that Grandma had yet to utter a single syllable of complaint.

She observed the town carefully. At least fifty buildings clustered together. Wow. This place was a veritable metropolis after Acuna. "Do you know someone here?" she asked Grandma. "Someone we can spend the night with?"

Grandma frowned. "This is an army town."

Which meant there would be eyes and informants aplenty. Elise's heart sank. What had been the point of their long trek if this place was no safer than Acuna?

"We shall put ourselves in the hands of our heavenly Father," Grandma intoned.

Elise stifled a groan. Faith was one thing. But blind faith was just irritating. They were on their own to use their wits to save themselves. Grandma was marching resolutely toward the village, however, and Elise highly doubted she could say anything to talk the woman out of whatever she had planned. Huffing in resignation, Elise followed after the woman and the children. She'd just have to brazen out whatever disaster Grandma's faith led them into.

It figured. The town had a Catholic church. Well, a teeny little chapel, to be more accurate. But it had four walls to go with its roof, which many churches in this part of the world did not. It looked old. Spanish in architecture. It was actually a pretty little place.

They stepped inside. Elise was startled at the sense of quiet peace pervading the space. It reminded her of Our Lady of Sacred Hope back in New York. Predictably, the chapel held rows of wooden pews and a large table covered in white cloth for an altar. A simple wooden crucifix hung on the front wall.

Grandma stopped to genuflect, and Elise followed suit behind her, trying to remember how Father Ambrose did it back home. She was so busted if the older woman asked her to recite a Mass or something like that. But thankfully, the older woman merely made her way forward, calling out for the priest.

Nobody answered.

"Does the local priest live near here?" Elise asked Grandma. Maybe she could have a private word with the man and explain who she was and why she was masquerading as a nun before he blew her cover.

"He travels from village to village."

Elise didn't know whether to be relieved or disappointed that they were own their own in the chapel.

"I'm hungry," Emanuel whined.

"Me, too," Mia piped up.

Both children had spotted the bowl of fruit sitting on the altar and were eyeing it longingly. Elise considered it, as well. Although offerings like that weren't specifically a Catholic ritual as far as she knew, the old customs of the Incan people had blended with Catholicism in this part of the world.

"I'm sure the Lord will not mind if we share his supper tonight," she murmured to them. She glanced hesitantly at Grandma, who nodded in agreement.

She felt like a heel for using her fake nun status to talk them into what was probably some terrible blasphemy. But they were all ravenous after the long hike, and it wasn't as if any of them could stroll out and buy dinner without having to answer a lot of questions. In a town this small, even Grandma would be identified quickly as an outsider.

As a sop to her guilt over stealing the offering for God, Elise added, "But first we have to say grace."

The children subsided and waited impatiently while she mumbled through a quick prayer blessing the food and thanking heavenly Father for his bounty. Darkness fell as they dug into the mangoes, guavas, bananas and black sapote—a local sweet fruit that tasted somewhat like a pomegranate. Moonlight filtered in through the small, high windows as the night grew cool.

The children stretched out on a pew, covered with Grandma's big shawl. They were being good sports about sleeping on the hard bench, and Elise's admiration for the children grew a notch. They were both bright and cooperative. She had to admit that whoever'd been raising Garza's children had done an excellent job of it so far.

Elise stationed herself by the back door to keep watch as Grandma dozed next to the kids. The town settled down to sleep, the car noises and the occasional sound of voices winding down and eventually ceasing. And that was why she jerked to full alertness at the abrupt sound of big engines—lots of them—rumbling into town a little before midnight.

Crud. That sounded almost like a convoy of some kind. What if the army had come looking for them? This was the closest town to Acuna and the logical place for them to have come. She glanced around the tiny chapel in panic. There was nowhere to hide. And she knew better than anyone how much the army respected the sanctity of the church. They'd barge right in here and slaughter her and the Garza children without a second thought. If only there were some sort of hidey-hole—

Father Ambrose told her once that most Catholic churches in olden times had a cellar of some kind. They'd been used over the centuries to hide all kinds of refugees, be they escaping slaves or the children of hated government strongmen. Was there any chance this little church was no exception? It did look fairly old and the decorations had a distinct Spanish flair.

What had Father Ambrose said? The cellars were usually near or under the altar section of the church, as this was the most holy and sacred portion of any church. She raced forward.

Grandma's eyes opened.

"The army's coming," Elise bit out. "We must hide." She lifted the linen tablecloth that draped to the floor to look for a trapdoor. But it was too dark for her to see a thing. She fell to her knees, running her hands over the floor desperately. There. A long, thin crack running perpendicular to the floorboards. The joints in the wood should be staggered, but weren't.

The sound of engines was audible inside the chapel now. Grandma woke the children, shushing them as they murmured sleepily.

Elise pried at the crack in the wood with her fingernails, but to no avail. It had to be some sort of trapdoor, but she had no idea how to open it. Which made sense. If it was a secret hiding place, it wouldn't open easily.

Grandma and the children knelt beside her.

"Get under the altar cloth," Elise whispered.

Shouting voices drifted in through the windows, and terror lined the children's faces in the faint moonlight. They were trapped, and all four of them knew it. They crawled under the table, but it would only provide a moment's additional protection.

"There's a trapdoor, but I can't open it," she breathed to Grandma.

Grandma whispered back, "Look for a hidden switch." The older woman joined her in frantically searching the floor with her hands.

Oh, God. Those were voices on the porch steps.

Mia pointed at the under side of the altar table. "What's that?"

Elise looked up. A small lever of some kind protruded faintly from the underside of the table nestled next to one of the table legs. Elise pushed it. Nothing. She wedged a finger under it and gave it a tug. A faint clicking noise sounded below them.

She scrabbled backward fast, moving her weight off what turned out to be the trapdoor. Her rear end stuck out from under the table toward the crucifix as she yanked the trapdoor up with strength born of panic. It opened upward on silent hinges.

The chapel door squeaked open. A man shouted orders to someone outside as the children headed down the narrow wooden steps. Grandma turned awkwardly, climbing down into the cellar with maddening slowness. Several men joined the first one, noisily moving into the chapel.

Flashlight beams glowed through the altar cloth as they searched the rows of pews. Elise scooted forward, flinging her feet down into the hole. She found a step with her feet and grabbed the trapdoor, pulling it down over her head frantically as she crouched on the step. Boots stomped into sight in the thin space visible beyond the altar cloth and a man spoke, no more than three feet away, as she eased the door fully closed.

It was stuffy and dusty and Elise jammed a hand over her nose as she felt a sneeze coming on. She held on to the door handle with her other hand and prayed the soldiers wouldn't find the latch Mia had spotted. And if they did spot it, maybe she could hold the door down and not give away their hiding spot.

She held her breath as she heard the altar cloth being ripped away. *Dear God, if You exist, and if You actually answer prayers, please don't let those soldiers spot the trapdoor.*

Ted crouched beside his Jeep on the outskirts of the town H.O.T. Watch had seen the refugees of Acuna headed for earlier. Colombian Army trucks were crisscrossing the place, turning people out of their homes and searching every building from top to bottom. Surely Elise and those two kids of hers weren't the object of such a determined search. But a sick feeling in his gut said they were. Who *were* those children?

If they were, indeed, Valdiron Garza's kids as Elise had all but admitted, why would the government be coming after them so hard? Although, a person had only to look at their father's deeds to deduce the answer to that one. Garza might have worked for the Colombian government, but even his own bosses had been terrified of him. Now that he was gone, everyone—within the government and without—was out to wipe away anything that had to do with him or his memory. Kind of like when Stalin died in Russia or Saddam Hussein in Iraq.

Ted was getting damned tired of being one step behind the army all the time like this. He hated having to sit here, helpless, and wait out the search. There was nothing for him to do but pray Elise and the kids weren't discovered or weren't here at all. When he caught up with her, he wasn't letting her out of his sight again for a good long time.

The search took over an hour, but he saw no commotions to indicate the army had found whoever they were looking for. They buzzed like angry bees as they headed for their vehicles and cleared out. The townspeople went back into their homes, and the night settled into silence once more.

Now, where would he go if he were a fake nun with two small children in tow? She didn't know anyone in town and she dared not stay at a hotel. Had she broken into a business and hidden there? Except the army had searched the stores in town. Thoroughly, if the shouts and complaints of the shopkeepers were any indication.

"Talk to me about this town," he muttered to the long-suffering duty controller at H.O.T. Watch.

"A thousand residents. Makes its legal income shipping local produce by river barge to the coast. Makes its real income refining cocaine. The populace is known to be loyal to the government."

Which explained why no residents had been shot during tonight's search. And which made it even more unlikely that Elise would've been hidden by anyone here, even if she was ostensibly a nun—

His train of thought derailed. A nun. Surely not. He spied the spire of the small church across town. It was as good a place as any to look. Although the army must have searched the place. What the heck. He might just be a little better than the local army guys at spotting a sexy nun with a couple of kids in tow.

Elise jerked fully awake as a loud squeaking sound erupted. That was the chapel's front door opening. The army couldn't have come back. A townsperson, maybe, coming to check on the church? Someone coming to pray? At this time of night? Nah. Who, then? She eased up the wooden steps and positioned herself directly under the trapdoor once more. She pulled down on the handle to keep it from popping open if this latest intruder knew about the hidden latch.

The children had been afraid of the total darkness down here in this crude dirt cellar and had wanted to go back up into the chapel to sleep. But now she was intensely relieved she'd insisted they spend the rest of the night down here. If they were lucky, the local priest would discover them tomorrow. Although, her luck hadn't been so great recently. Better safe than sorry.

The intruder was quiet, but in her hyperafraid state, she heard the faint whisper of fabric as he moved slowly through the chapel. Just as someone would if they were searching the place. He drew near the altar. She held her breath, even though there was no way he could hear her breathing through the thick wooden panel overhead.

The latch clicked, dammit. She hung on to the trapdoor as it would've popped slightly open and prayed the intruder gave up as quickly as the army had.

A whisper floated down to her. She couldn't quite hear it and rose up slightly to press her ear to the wood. There it was again.

"Elise?"

Her heart nearly stopped.

"It's me. Drago."

Ohmigod. She pushed the panel up and was startled when it didn't budge. Momentary panic that they were stuck down here flooded her. There was a grunt and then she realized he must be kneeling on the trapdoor. The panel flew up all of a sudden.

She rushed up the steps and into his arms, knocking him over on his back in her exuberance. "Thank God it's you. My prayers were answered."

He laughed quietly as she sprawled across his chest. "Hello to you, too."

Her relief was such that she kissed him soundly without thinking. His mouth was warm and firm beneath hers but went hot and demanding the instant their lips touched.

His arms came up around her while her hands slid up his chest to grip his shoulders. He hugged her so tightly she struggled to breathe. But she didn't mind. It felt so good to be held by someone that she all but purred aloud. Her mouth opened against his and he reciprocated immediately. Their tongues met and she slanted her mouth across his, engrossed in the dance of lips and teeth and tongues. One of his hands slid up underneath her hair to the back of her head, cupping it so he could explore even more deeply. She gave in eagerly, melting against him as he took charge of the kiss.

She writhed against him, her body on fire. He groaned in the back of his throat and she reveled in the sound. She did that to him? Cool. She kissed him with renewed enthusiasm. She wanted to hear that sound again.

He was the one who finally broke off the kiss, breathing heavily. His heart pounded against her chest, matching her galloping pulse.

"I'm so glad to see you," she chattered under her breath. "Here I was trying to figure out how we were going to get out of this town without someone turning us in to the army. And then you just showed up. How did you find us, anyway? Is it safe? Can we leave now? Do you have a car?"

"And you accuse me of asking a lot of questions," he muttered around a grin.

"Well?" she demanded.

"Yes, we're safe. The army has cleared out for the moment. You don't want to know how I found you, yes we can leave now, and of course I have wheels. Do you have the children?"

"I do. And Grandma."

He blinked up at her.

"Speaking of which." She called out low in Spanish, "He's a friend. You can come out."

Grandma poked her head up out of the hidey-hole as Elise hastily rolled off his totally delicious chest. She felt bereft as his arms fell away from her and he sat up. He held a hand forward to help the elderly woman climb out of the cellar. Grandma rolled awkwardly to her hands and knees and asked, "Is it safe?"

Drago nodded. "Here. Let me help you up." He crawled out from under the table and partially lifted Grandma to her feet while Elise smiled down at the two small, pale faces peering up out of the hole.

"This is my good friend, Drago. He's come to help us."

"Is he one of the superheroes?" Emanuel asked, eyeing the humongous gun slung over Drago's shoulder in awe.

"He sure is," Elise replied jauntily.

She made the introductions quickly and was startled when, after high-fiving Emanuel, he knelt down on one knee to shake Mia's hand solemnly. The little girl seemed charmed in spite of herself. Who'd have guessed the big, bad arms dealer would be so good with children? Bemused, she introduced him to Grandma, who eyed him with open appreciation.

His gaze met hers over the older woman's head, and his eyes glinted with humor.

Elise commented in English, "Like she told me earlier, she's not dead yet."

Drago laughed, retorting, "I always say, when I quit looking, bury me because I'm dead."

"Where's your car?" Elise asked more seriously.

He flipped into work mode immediately. "Outside. Lemme clear the area and then I'll wave you out. Have you got any stuff?"

"Just a few emergency supplies Grandma had in a bag."

"Smart woman." He nodded and melted out into the night. He did that so easily. Her suspicion that he was much more than a simple arms dealer resurfaced with a vengeance. Of course, the moment she started asking questions about who he really was, he would do the same to her. She was actually grateful for a moment that they still weren't out of danger. The longer she could avoid the hard questions waiting for her from Drago, the better.

He waved to her, and Elise hustled Grandma and the kids out to his Jeep. They piled in the backseat and she climbed in the passenger seat beside him. He started the car but left the headlights off.

He quietly directed Grandma and the children to lie down in the backseat and cover themselves with Grandma's shawl. She was startled to see how carefully he lifted the children and how gently he tucked a blanket around them to hide them.

Elise murmured, "And I suppose you want me to get down on the floor?"

He answered in English, "I was thinking more in terms

of you lying down with your head in my lap, but I suppose the floor works."

"You wish." Grinning, she wedged herself between the dashboard and her seat.

"It would've been more comfortable my way," he commented.

"Not when I was through with you it wouldn't have," she blurted without thinking. His gaze snapped to hers. Whoops.

"I'm exhausted," she muttered. "I don't know what I'm saying."

His gaze narrowed speculatively and she swore under her breath. He didn't buy her excuse for a second. She was the worst fake nun ever! She watched apprehensively as he nodded to himself and then threw her another one of those "we need to talk" looks.

As she crouched on the floor, her legs started to tingle and then to ache, but she'd be twice damned before she complained about her cramped position. Finally, he turned on the headlights and announced that everyone could sit up. She pulled herself back into the passenger seat gratefully.

They drove on a two-lane paved road for hours. Although, the existence of asphalt didn't prevent the road from having gargantuan ruts and potholes that could swallow a small house. It was slow going, particularly after the moon set and heavy darkness fell outside.

Grandma and the children crashed in the backseat and Elise grew sleepy. She murmured to Drago, "If you're tired I don't mind driving for a while."

He shook his head. "I've got it."

"You know, I've worked plenty of double shifts in emergency rooms. I can go twenty-four hours or more if I have to."

"You don't have to," he replied.

"Are you one of those macho men who insists on taking care of the woman all the time?"

"You don't have to make that sound like some terrible character flaw."

"So you *are* a Neanderthal?"

"I'm a gentleman. I was raised to believe that the man takes care of the women and children. Keeps them safe. Looks out for them."

He was a dealer in death. Since when did notions like protecting the weak and helpless enter into that equation? "Do you go for the whole opening doors and holding chairs thing, too?" she asked curiously.

"I do," he bit out.

Huh. She'd heard of men like him—old-fashioned types who held with values like courtesy and chivalry—but she couldn't remember the last time she'd met one. He couldn't be for real, could he? "And do you hunt saber-toothed tigers with a club and drag the woman off by the hair to your cave?"

He glanced over at her and shrugged. "I'm old-school. I freely admit that. If you're the kind of woman who likes it, great. If not, then we can go our separate ways, no harm, no foul."

Honesty compelled her to confess, "I don't know if I like it or not. I've never known a man who felt that way."

"Seriously?" he blurted.

"As a heart attack. I spend most of my time trolling the worst neighborhoods New York City has to offer. I'm just glad when the men there don't shoot me." Although, now that she thought about it, she supposed many of the men did look out for her in their own rough fashion in the form of gang escorts and repeated attempts to teach her how to shoot a gun.

"Why do you run around in such bad places and endanger yourself?" Drago asked in audible alarm.

"I'm a nurse. Many of my patients can't or won't seek medical care unless it comes to them."

He shook his head. "You should have someone like me along with you to look out for you."

"Are you volunteering for the job?" Good grief. She had to quit spilling out the first words that came to her head like that.

He frowned. "Unfortunately, I have other commitments. But if I didn't, yeah, sure. I'd watch your back."

"I don't think most nuns have bodyguards," she replied.

"But you're not most nuns, now are you?"

Her gaze snapped to him, but he was staring straight ahead at the road. His profile was strong. Clean. Well-defined. And it didn't give away even a hint of what he meant by that remark.

Even if he wouldn't let her take a turn driving, she stubbornly insisted on staying awake with him through the night and keeping him company. He seemed amused that she thought he wouldn't be able to remain alert all by himself.

Finally, as the sky began to lighten in the east behind them, he said, "Why don't you close your eyes for a few minutes? You've had a rough couple of days."

Now that was an understatement. But at least she had Mia and Emanuel now, and could turn her attention to getting out of this godforsaken region. "I'll be fine," she replied stubbornly.

"It's getting light out. I'll be good to go for most of the day. Take a nap."

She retorted, "Look. If it's all right for you to take care of the weak, helpless female, it's also all right for me to worry about you."

He looked startled. "There's no reason for you to worry about me. I've got things handled."

"Then why are we headed into the heart of Army of Freedom territory? You do realize we could be jumped at any moment, right?"

"Actually, I'm hoping they do jump us. I've got to get back into contact with Raoul and company so I can complete my deal with them."

Elise's jaw dropped. "You *want* to find those cutthroats?"

"Absolutely."

"News flash. You've two women and two small children with you now. None of us needs to be exposed to a bunch of violent insurgents."

"Do you want me to pull over and let all of you out of the car?" he asked.

"No! I want you to drive us to some nice, big, safe city with an international airport so I can get these kids out of Colombia."

"I'll be happy to do that…after I close my sale."

"Your sale is immoral."

He snorted. "Like you're one to comment on my morality."

What did he mean by that? Sure, she wasn't a great fake nun. But she hadn't done anything to really disgrace the profession, had she? Kissing him probably hadn't been strictly nunlike, but she couldn't help it. He kept catching her at weak moments. And besides…he was hot.

They drove in silence as the sun rose and the thin layer of ground fog burned off, leaving the young day hazy and humid, promising hellish heat by afternoon. The jungle gave way to rolling grassland, and ranches and farms became more and more prevalent. They stopped in a village to refuel, use restrooms and eat breakfast. Drago stocked up on snacks and drinking water, as well.

Elise spent the rest of the morning cooking up games to play with the children to pass the time. The children dozed again in the early afternoon, and since Drago really did appear to be going strong, she finally allowed herself to close her eyes.

It was nearly dark when she blinked awake, her neck stiff and her back aching.

"Good evening, Sleeping Beauty," Drago murmured.

"Good grief! You let me sleep the whole afternoon away!"

"You needed it. Grandma read a book I picked up in that village to the munchkins, and listening to it kept me wide awake. No reason for you not to sleep for a while."

She supposed there was no sense in crying over spilled milk. The nap was a done deal and she felt worlds better. "So, are you going to let me drive now that I've had some sleep and you haven't?"

"Nope."

"Has anyone ever told you you're insanely stubborn?"

He blinked innocently at her. "Why, whatever do you mean?"

She didn't know whether to scowl or laugh at him. She settled for huffing in exasperation. "You're such a…"

"Man?" he offered.

"Exactly."

He chuckled. "Thanks."

"It wasn't a compliment," she snapped.

"Yeah, I got that memo. But thanks, anyway."

"Ooh!"

"You're so cute when you're mad. You look like a kitten who's being tewwibwy fewocious and is about to attack a ball of yarn."

"Yeah, well, kittens can tear up a ball of yarn with the best of them. Don't underestimate my claws, mister."

He smiled indulgently. "It's not your claws that are the problem. It's that stubborn determination of yours that'll get you in trouble."

Actually, he was right. But there was no way on God's green earth she would admit that to him.

The road quality improved dramatically through the Llanos—the tropical grasslands bordering the majestic Orinoco River. They drove at near highway speed until the foothills of the Andes Mountains began to rise around them. By her calculation, the road trip had taken them nearly halfway across the country. Now all she had to do was make her way to the coast and a major airport. There had to be a way for her to return to the States without her passport, and in the meantime, Mia and Emanuel would be safe once she got them on a plane.

They stopped and made a picnic supper of the food Drago'd had the foresight to purchase. After the meal, from somewhere in the back of the vehicle, a soccer ball mysteriously emerged. Emanuel shouted with delight, and she smiled gratefully at Drago. You had to love a man who went out of his way like that to make a little kid happy.

Whoa. Love? Huh. Maybe she did love him just a little.

He looked away guiltily. What? The big bad arms dealer didn't want her to know he had a soft spot for kids? If only he knew how much sexier it made him—she broke off the thought in sharp frustration. If nothing else, this disastrous nun disguise had taught her once and for all that a celibate lifestyle was *not* for her.

Elise and Grandma watched the boys pass the ball back and forth. But then Drago did something surprising. He kicked the ball to Mia where she slouched beside the Jeep. The little girl reluctantly kicked the ball back. How he pulled it off, Elise wasn't quite sure, but within a few minutes, he'd coaxed Mia into the action. The two children squealed with laughter at Drago's ridiculous antics as they played keep-away from him. Her heart melted a little bit more.

Grandma murmured, "He will make a good father. And so handsome, he is. A girl would be crazy to let him go."

Elise glanced over at the elderly woman in surprise. Surely Grandma wasn't advocating that a nun cast off the cloth and her vows for the hunky arms dealer! Unless… crud…Grandma'd figured out she wasn't really a nun. But how? Elise thought back frantically over the past day. How had she given herself away?

Drago interrupted her silent panic by flopping down on the grass beside her.

"They wear you out?" Elise asked him.

He snorted. "It takes more than jumping around like a monkey for a few minutes to tire me out."

"Where did you learn to handle children so well?"

"Me?" He looked startled. "I don't know the first thing about kids."

"Could've fooled me. You don't have any of your own?"

"Not that I'm aware of," he answered sharply.

"No nieces and nephews you spoil rotten when you go home?"

"No."

"Where is home, anyway?"

"I told you. France."

Yeah, right. And she was the Easter Bunny. "Well, regardless, you're a natural with kids. You should have a bunch of your own someday."

Alarm bordering on panic passed across his face. "Impossible."

"Why not?"

He glanced over at the children, who were still kicking the ball back and forth. "Look what happened to them. Their father was in a violent business and got himself killed. And where did it leave them? Running for their lives through no fault of their own."

Guilt speared through her. Memory of her persistent calls to congressmen, journalists and various international human rights groups flashed through her mind. She'd been one of the main reasons Garza's violence had finally been exposed. She might not have pulled the trigger of the gun that killed him, but she'd darn well painted the target on his back.

She glanced over at Drago. "So you'd never consider leaving the arms business to pursue more peaceful endeavors?"

He shrugged. "Once you've made the kind of enemies I have, peace isn't in the cards. The best I could hope for is to lie low long enough that my enemies eventually forget about me."

"That doesn't sound impossible."

He shredded a long stem of grass into tiny bits and announced bitterly, "No woman would agree to living in danger for years just to be with me."

"I would."

She swore at herself. Had those words just come out of her mouth? She stood up hastily, studiously avoiding meeting his eyes as she gathered the remains of their meal and stuffed the trash into a plastic grocery bag. But oh, how she felt his gaze upon her, watching her every move with hawklike attention. *She would not look at him. She would not look at him....*

At the end of the day, it wasn't as though she should or would find happiness, herself. After abandoning her parents, blithely going out to pursue her own fun and leaving them behind to die, she didn't deserve an instant of joy for the rest of her life.

The children reluctantly ended their play at Drago's quiet declaration that it was time to go. She had to give the kids credit for having been tremendously patient about being cooped up so long in the backseat of a car. Hopefully, they were too young to understand the danger they'd been in yesterday, but she feared they were fully aware of how close to dying they had come.

Mia and Emanuel had no more choice about who their father was and what he'd done than she did. She had that in common with them, too. All three of them were victims of Valdiron Garza.

Grandma was stoic about the loss of her home. She'd been penniless and displaced before, apparently. She seemed to grasp that being alive and safe was what truly mattered. All the creature comforts and possessions could be replaced. Elise knew better than most that family could not be replaced, however.

The children came over to the Jeep, panting, and Drago loaded them into the vehicle with quick ruffles of their hair that brought smiles to the children's faces. Yup, a natural with kids.

"How much longer are you planning to drive?" Elise asked him.

"Until the Army of Freedom finds us."

"What if they don't?"

"Then I guess I'll have to find them."

"With all of us in tow?"

"Tell me where you'd like me to drop you off—someplace that's reasonably safe—and I'll be happy to oblige you."

Elise sighed. No place in Colombia was safe for the Garza children. Their father had terrorized people from one end of the country to the other. Her original plan was still the best one: make for a city with an international airport and get the heck out of Dodge.

Grandma spoke up from the backseat. "You wish to find the Army of Freedom?"

Elise turned around, surprised. "Do you know how to do that?"

"Of course. My son and daughter are both freedom fighters. Go to Mercado. There's a hotel called La Guarida del Diablo."

"The Devil's Den?" Elise muttered in English. "Well, isn't that just cheerful?"

Drago snorted beside her.

"Do you know it?" she asked him.

"How hard can it be to find with a name like that? Everyone for miles around will know where it is."

"Do you know where Mercado is?" Elise asked. She opened the glove compartment in search of a map but found none.

"Nope, but I can find out." He pulled out a cell phone and held it to his ear.

"I need directions to Mercado." He listened for several moments and then disconnected.

How did he do that? How did the person on the other end of the phone know where Drago was right now to be able to rattle off directions to some village? It wasn't as if the various high-end satellite tracking services in the United States were available in an isolated place like this. "Who was that?" Elise demanded.

"A friend."

"How did your friend know where you are?"

Drago frowned and didn't answer.

"I'm not stupid. How did whoever you called know where we are? Who's watching us?"

"No one you need to worry about."

"I don't buy it. I'm responsible for two children and one elderly lady. I have a right to know."

"Oh, and now you're responsible for Grandma, too?"

"Yes, I am. She was looking out for the kids when her home was burned down and she lost everything she owns. It's the least I can do for her."

"She was in the wrong village at the wrong time. Unless—" Drago glanced over at her keenly "—you think the children were the reason for the army attack and not the rebel patrol in the area."

"It had to be the Army of Freedom. They're just orphans."

"Are they really Garza's kids?"

She swore mentally. "I'm not at liberty to say."

He pressed his lips together and she did the same. They both had their own secrets to guard. The day's easy camaraderie evaporated, leaving behind tense silence between them.

Finally, when she couldn't stand the suspense any longer, she asked tightly, "How far to Mercado?"

"A half hour if the road holds up."

A half hour until they would part ways, most likely never to see each other again. As infuriating as he might be with his secrets and macho attitude, sharp regret pierced her annoyance. In a different time, different circumstances, they might have had something special between them. As slowly as the minutes and miles had crawled all day, they flew past that quickly now.

There had to be something she could say. Some way to break through the stony silence he'd pulled around himself like a fortress. But she was supposed to be a nun. It wasn't as though she could hand him her phone number with an admonition to give her a call sometime. Besides, the guy was an illegal arms dealer, for crying out loud. She had no interest in entangling herself in a world of crime and violence. No man was worth dying for.

Lights began to twinkle ahead of them. Mercado. They would arrive in just a few minutes. A vague sense of panic hovered at the edge of her consciousness. It was a mistake to let this man slip out of her life. But what could she do? It boiled down to a choice between jeopardizing the children's safety by revealing her nun ruse and her lust for a hot arms dealer. The right decision was a no-brainer.

The Jeep slowed and pulled over to the side of the road beneath a cluster of trees. Drago turned off the headlights and the ignition.

"What are we doing?" she asked in alarm.

"You and I are getting out of the car for a minute."

"Why?" she demanded, her voice squeaking in alarm.

"We need to have a conversation. In private."

# Chapter 9

Ted was surprised when Elise actually climbed out of the Jeep, albeit with obvious reluctance. He murmured an excuse to Grandma about needing to discuss possible dangers ahead and not wanting to frighten the children. The older woman's gaze shifted back and forth between him and Elise. Crud. She didn't look like she bought his excuse. Sharp old bird, she was.

He turned off his cell phone and murmured into the concealed microphone sewn into his collar, "Turn off the recorders for a minute. This is private."

"Excuse me?" Elise asked as she came around the end of the vehicle.

"Nothing," he mumbled. He took her by the elbow and led her deeper into the trees, no more than a dozen yards from the Jeep, but completely out of sight of its dark silhouette.

He turned to face her and she took an immediate step back, crossing her arms across her chest defensively.

"Don't you think it's time we had a frank conversation with each other?" he asked quietly.

"Not at all. I've got nothing to be frank about, thank you very much."

"Perhaps you'd like to explain to me why you're pretending to be a nun?"

"Pretending…why, I…how dare—"

He cut her off. "Give it up. There's no way a nun would kiss me like you did. Twice."

"The first time was your fault. The second time was merely…overflowing relief."

"So you're trying to tell me that our kisses had no effect on you? That you don't want to do it again and you're willing to walk away from whatever this is between us?"

"I—" She ground to a halt.

He had to give her credit for not being comfortable with lying. She was trying to be as honest as she could within the confines of her disguise. And hey. At least she was hesitating at the idea of walking away from him. That was good news—

Wait a minute. What the hell was he thinking? That wasn't good at all! He was a Special Forces operator in the middle of an incredibly dangerous and sensitive mission. Brady Hathaway would have his head on a platter if he screwed this up because of a woman, no matter how flaming a do-gooder she was.

"…fine," she was saying. "You caught me. I confess I'm guilty of having impure thoughts. I'll go to confession when I get home and will no doubt do penance for the next twenty years. But that's between me and my priest."

He chuckled. "Impure thoughts? Honey, you kiss like you were made for sin."

It was too dark to see much, but she looked a bit overheated all of a sudden. She spoke calmly enough when she replied, though. "We've been over this before. In spite of my profession, I am in fact a female and human, and subject to the same…urges…as any other woman."

"So you deny that you find me as irresistible as I find you?"

"Irresistible?" she echoed faintly.

"That's right," he answered firmly. "Admit it. You're no more a nun than I am."

"How dare you—"

He held up a hand, cutting off her protest. "Enough with the flimsy disguise, already." Time was growing short, and he wasn't getting back in the car until they'd cut through all the crap and gotten to the truth.

"But—"

"Care to kiss me again and prove that you don't feel a thing when we do it?" Her eyes blazed. But with lust or fury, he couldn't tell. "Go on, Elise. I dare you. Kiss me."

"And then you'll drop this line of questioning once and for all?"

"What the heck. Sure."

She stepped forward, a determined glint in her eyes. Desire leaped in his gut all of a sudden. This should be interesting. She put a hand on his chest, incinerating the spot over his heart with her soft touch. He watched her with predatory eyes as she stood on tiptoe and pecked him on the mouth with tightly pursed lips so quickly he barely felt it.

She stumbled back as if he'd burned her and he grinned. "That wasn't a kiss, darlin', and you know it."

She huffed. "You're enjoying torturing me, aren't you? People go to hell for less, you know."

His grin widened. "I'm waiting."

"You are insufferable."

"Too much talking. Not enough kissing."

"Ooh," she growled. "What did I ever see in you?"

"I dunno. Kiss me and find out."

"One kiss. And then you'll drop the subject forever."

"Correct."

She stepped forward again, this time with a great deal more trepidation. Smart girl. Standing on tiptoe once more, she looped her slender arms over his shoulders and tugged on his head, bringing it down toward her. Their lips met and an artillery barrage exploded inside his head, complete with blinding tracers and screaming explosions of incoming fire.

His arms swept around her and she moaned into his mouth, melting into him and over him until he didn't know where he ended and she began. She tasted better than any woman had a right to and he drew her higher against his body as she invited him in with her entire being.

Their tongues clashed, quickly finding a rhythm that made his entire body throb with need. She gasped but never broke the contact. Her words might vow to push him away, but her hands urged him closer, pulling on the back of his neck urgently, drawing him down to her. And he had no will to resist. He picked her up completely off the ground, supporting her slight weight with ease. Her arms went fully around his neck then, her head slanting to give him even deeper access to her mouth, which he didn't hesitate to exploit.

The lust that simmered beneath the surface all the time when he was around her broke loose, rolling over him until he gasped with the power of it. She must have felt it, too, for she surged against him with a cry in the back of her throat that owed nothing to piety and everything to unbridled desire. The urge to protect and possess that he'd fought ever since he met her reared up again. This was his woman, end of discussion. The only question was how long it would take her to admit it.

He backed her up, standing her on a small fallen log to compensate for their height difference and freeing his hands to roam over her delicious body, learning her. Marking her as his. Now, here was something he could do for the rest of his life. The idea galvanized him. Was it possible? Could he actually find someone who'd be willing to put up with him and his emotional baggage? Hope erupted in his chest.

But then Elise distracted him by shivering beneath his touch, so sensitive he reeled with the possibilities of how she'd react if there were no clothes between his palms and her skin. His hands slid under her sweater, but that awful dress of hers gave him no access to anything other than her bare arms. At least the fabric was thin enough for her heat to pass through it and hint at goose bumps puckering her delicate flesh.

She was as responsive as the finest musical instrument to his touch, a veritable symphony of tiny sounds escaping her throat as he stroked her to a fever pitch. The sweet smell of her wreathed them both, and he inhaled it with the same fierce possessiveness that he inhaled all of her. A single word echoed through his besotted brain. *Mine.*

She grew ever more soft and boneless against him, trembling so much with desire that he had to wrap his arms around her once more to steady her. She finally dragged her mouth away from his and buried her face against his neck, trembling. Her hair smelled like her, and he memorized the soft scent while she panted against him.

"Don't say it," she murmured, her mouth moving tantalizingly against his bare skin above his collar.

"Don't say what?" He was surprised to hear how breathless he was, too.

"I told you so."

He laughed silently. "Ready to admit you want me?"

He felt her sigh. "Fine. I want you."

"And you're not a nun."

She pursed her lips stubbornly at that one, but the truth was easy to read in her eyes.

"You're a terrible liar," he murmured. "I can see it in your eyes, so why don't you just admit it? I swear I mean you no harm."

Another sigh, this one longer and more drawn out. "Fine. I'm not a nun." But then she added in a rush, "You have to promise me you won't tell anybody. Not a soul. I have to get Mia and Emanuel out of Colombia safely, and being a nun is the best and fastest way to do that. Their safety depends on you keeping the secret."

"I already figured out that was why you were pretending to be a sister, and I haven't given you away, yet."

"Promise me you won't tell."

He put a finger under her chin and tipped her face up to his gently. "I promise." He sealed the promise with a kiss. He intended for it to be a chaste thing, no more than an affirmation of his promise, but he should have known better. As soon as their mouths met again, this time without the thin veil of pretense that she wasn't supposed to enjoy this, an entire battlefield of heat and fury ignited between them.

He tugged at the front of her dress, impatient with the frumpy garment. Fumbling hastily, she undid the buttons in a clumsy effort to save them from his assault. And then his hands were finally on her skin, skimming over her entirely immodest lace bra and tracing the indent of her tiny waist.

His mouth dropped to her bare shoulder. He followed the path of her collarbone to where it ended at her throat.

He sipped at the hollow there as she threw her head back to give him full access. And then his mouth tracked lower, dipping into the valley between her breasts. His hands went behind her, lifting her, arching her into his mouth wantonly.

Her hands clutched at his short hair, pressing him closer while she urged him on with pants of pleasure. "Oh, yes. More. Right there. I've wanted you so much!"

He knew the feeling. As much as he'd love to carry her down to the forest floor and make love to her right now, she deserved better. She deserved satin sheets and rose petals, soft music and champagne. Reluctantly, he kissed his way back up the soft vulnerability of her neck to her mouth.

"I'll never get enough of you," he whispered against her lips.

"Then tell me something," she murmured back between kisses. "Who are you?"

Elise felt Drago freeze against her. Retreat emotionally. Quickly and completely.

"Oh, come on, Drago. What's good for the goose is good for the gander. I've entrusted you with my big secret. You can share yours with me. Who are you and what are you really doing out here?"

"What do you mean?" he asked cautiously, standing upright and reaching out to button her dress.

"You're more than just some simple arms dealer."

"Why do you think that?"

He was back to being Mr. All-Questions-and-No-Answers again. "You went out of your way to help some crazy nun who wandered across your path. You didn't have to come to Acuna to rescue me and the kids, but you did. You obviously like the children and are going out of your way to be kind to them. By coming after us, you lost contact with a potentially lucrative client. What arms dealer in their right mind would do that?"

"One with a soft spot for crazy nuns and helpless kids?"

"Nice try, but no cigar," she retorted. "What gives?"

"I can't tell you."

"Why not?"

"My secrets are bigger than yours."

She snorted. "That's a load of hooey. What's more important than the lives of two innocent children?"

He answered without hesitation. "The lives of hundreds of innocent children."

"Huh?"

"Like I said. Don't ask."

"I'm asking." He started to turn away, to shut her out. She added desperately, "If what we have between us means anything at all to you, you'll tell me. You owe me that much."

He turned back to her and passed a frustrated hand over his face. "That's not fair."

"If I were a nun, I might fight fair. But I'm a woman. And since when do we ever fight fair?"

"Good point."

"Come on, Drago. Tell me."

"No."

And with that single word, uttered with quiet finality, he'd shut her out of his life.

Worse, she knew without a shadow of a doubt that there wasn't a darned thing she could do to change his mind or force him to spill his guts. His job—his secrets—were more important to him than she would ever be. And that pretty much said it all.

No matter how great her fantasies were of the two of them together after this trip, with her emphatically not posing as a nun, they were just that. Fantasies. They would never become a reality. He might kiss her as though he needed her more than life, but it was all just empty promises.

Devastated, she followed him back to the Jeep. She avoided Grandma's all-too-observant gaze and climbed into the passenger seat in silence. For once, she was glad to have the drab clothes and wimple to hide behind. It wasn't Drago's questions she feared anymore, though; it was Grandma's. Folding her hands as if in prayer, Elise bowed her head and closed her eyes. It was a close thing to fight off the tears burning the back of her eyelids, but she eventually managed to squeeze them away hard enough for her to open her eyes and actually see the road.

She glanced up and Grandma caught her gaze in the rearview mirror, the dark, wise eyes worried. "Are you all right, Sister Elise?"

"I am now. Prayer always calms me."

A shadow of doubt passed over the old woman's wrinkled face.

Elise said brightly, "In the few minutes we have left before we get to Mercado, we should probably strategize how to approach Raoul again and explain our absence."

"Who's he?" the older woman asked.

Drago answered, "The leader of the Army of Freedom."

Grandma frowned. "What are you talking about? Eduardo Lentano is the leader of the Army of Freedom."

Drago's head whipped around. His voice was deadly quiet. "Excuse me?"

# Chapter 10

Elise gulped. Was the Army of Freedom playing him for a fool? Just how much danger were they all in? "Uh, maybe you should reconsider the whole idea of getting us picked up by the rebels."

He shook his head. "No. We continue on. I have to finish this deal."

"No, you don't. You can walk away from this." When he merely scowled stubbornly, she added desperately, "Have you not looked around you? You have a car full of women and children."

He shrugged. "You can leave me when we get to Mercado, or you can take your chances with me. But I have no choice. Particularly now that I know they're messing with me. I must continue my mission."

His *mission?* What was he? Some kind of soldier? Or a spy, maybe?

Grandma surprised her by speaking up from the backseat. "I stay with the children. And they should stay with you, Drago. You know how to handle yourself. You'll protect them with your life."

An array of emotions passed across his face. Surprise. Dismay. Resignation. And then a reluctant smile of reassurance toward the elderly woman in the backseat. Did she dare interpret that to mean he'd accepted the fact that he was stuck with all of them until they left Colombia?

She didn't know whether to be relieved or appalled. Assuming he didn't draw the entire Army of Freedom down upon them, he might actually increase the children's safety. But he'd made it clear that his goals came before any women and children. Did she dare trust him? Did she have the right to risk the children's lives on his tenuous connection to them? Particularly after he'd made it crystal clear to her that the mission came first?

Hurt tore through her, paralyzing her brain. She had to *think*. Make the right decision. The children's safety, not to mention her own safety, depended on her making the right choice. But what was that?

"What more can you tell me about the Army of Freedom?" he asked Grandma quietly.

"They struggle to survive. The government's reforms are working. The cruelty and corruption of the regime have mostly disappeared. That is what drove people into rebel groups. With *el Presidente* giving back the farmland the drug cartels stole, the Army of Freedom can't even find supporters among the poorest people in the countryside."

"Are you telling me the Army of Freedom is dying?" he asked carefully.

"They used to have nearly ten thousand members. Now they're down to maybe five hundred."

"So few?" Drago blurted.

"Aye."

"So. They'd rather go out in a blaze of glory than fade quietly into the night," he mumbled.

"Excuse me?" Elise asked. She didn't like the sound of that. In her experience, blazes of glory had a tendency to consume anyone standing near them when they ignited.

"Nothing," he snapped, obviously distracted.

"Are you sure you want to go through with this arms deal?" she asked. "What if they can't pay you? Or what if they're planning to do something stupid with your weapons? Won't the authorities come after you, too?"

"This isn't about talking me out of doing business with these guys."

"What is it about, then?" she asked.

He glanced at her, his expression closed, and did not answer. Yup, he had shut her out completely.

"I don't want to approach them tonight," Drago announced suddenly. "We'll find a place to stay and I'll approach them—by myself—tomorrow."

Elise snorted. Which was a fancy way of saying he was going to ditch them tomorrow. How could he promise in one breath to keep them safe, and in the next intimate that he'd like nothing better than to get rid of them? His mood swings were giving her whiplash.

He pulled into a motel that was part of a major chain and got them three rooms connected by interior doors. At his suggestion, Grandma and the kids took the middle room, and he and Elise took the rooms on either side. He said it was for safety, but she suspected it had more to do with avoiding her and her inconvenient questions.

The children jumped on the beds and took baths and gleefully settled in to watch a children's movie on pay-per-view. Elise left Grandma dozing in the other double bed and tiptoed back to her room after the children nodded off, their faces untroubled and angelic in sleep.

Elise tossed and turned in her own bed for perhaps an hour when a quiet knock on her door brought her flying out of bed in alarm. She moved over to the door and spied Drago's distorted form through the peephole.

She opened the door a crack and whispered, "What do you want?"

"I want to talk."

Huh? She threw the door open and stepped back, confused. Her room had one large bed in it, and she sat down gingerly on its edge. Drago seated himself beside her, their knees disturbingly close. Sheesh. Since when had *knees* become an irresistibly erogenous zone?

He asked without preamble, "Do you believe in God?"

She stared at him. "What does that have to do with anything?"

"Do you ever think about hell?"

What on earth prompted that line of reasoning? Had her continuous criticisms of his profession finally gotten through to him? Maybe she didn't make such a bad nun after all. And maybe that was why she felt compelled to answer him with brutal honesty. "I don't think about hell now as much as I used to. There was a time when I thought about it a lot."

She stopped, but the almost desperate look he sent her spurred her to take a deep breath and plunge on. "I was in a pretty bad place emotionally right after my parents died. I considered coming down here to kill Garza, and I briefly considered killing myself. Either way, I figured I was going to end up in hell. Why do you ask?"

"Seeing Mia and Emanuel and what they've been through, I guess it messed with my head a little."

Surprise coursed through her. He'd given no indication

earlier that the children made him uncomfortable. Quite the opposite, in fact. Given how macho a guy he usually was, the admission that two little kids had gotten under his skin had to have cost him a lot.

"Messed with your head how?" she asked cautiously.

"In my line of work, I do the job and move on. I don't stick around to see the consequences of what I do. I've never really thought much about making orphans and widows." He shrugged. "I always put it down to collateral damage of what had to be done."

She nodded slowly. "I know the feeling."

His gaze jerked up to hers.

"After Valdiron Garza murdered my parents, I moved heaven and earth to see him brought to justice. I worked for years to expose his dirty activities and force the Colombian government to do something about him. I never dreamed they'd shoot him down in cold blood, though. In my own way, I'm as responsible for making orphans out of Mia and Emanuel as you are."

He nodded slowly. "Is that why you're here to rescue them?"

"I didn't know it when I agreed to come down here to get them, but yes, it's why I'm here."

Silence fell between them.

Eventually, she asked quietly, "Why do you do what you do? Is it for the money?"

He snorted. "Hell, no. Nobody gets rich doing what I do unless they go—"

They go *what?* As far as she knew, arms dealers were usually rolling in cash. Given that he struck her as being very good at what he did, she had to assume, then, that if he wasn't rich, it wasn't because he sucked at being an arms dealer. It had to be something else. Was he, in fact, a soldier of some kind? A spy, maybe?

Right. Like he'd ever tell her something like that. Rather than confronting him with it again and getting yet another denial from him, she chose a different tack. "What would you die for, Drago?"

He looked up at her sharply. "Excuse me?"

"What's worth dying for to you?"

He opened his mouth as if an answer came readily to him, but no words came out. Finally, he said lamely, "Family and friends, I suppose."

That wasn't what he'd been about to say. She'd lay odds that something like God and country was what leaped to his tongue first. "Look. I know you don't want to tell me who you really are. Maybe you can't tell me. I get that. But I have a pretty good idea who you might be. Which makes me wonder why you're out here all by yourself messing around with people like the Army of Freedom. Shouldn't you have some sort of backup? Someone waiting nearby to pull you out if things go to hell?"

His answer was slow in coming. Reluctant. "I'm on my own. No backup."

"What kind of idiot sends someone like you into this sort of danger alone?" she demanded indignantly.

He snorted. "Like you're one to talk. I don't see the Catholic cavalry standing in the wings waiting to swoop in and rescue you when you get in over your head."

She sighed. "Yes, but I volunteered for this. You could say I even brought it on myself. Penance, as it were."

He burst out, "That's insane." The vehemence in his voice startled her. It almost sounded as though he cared about her.

"Probably."

"Go home, Elise."

She laughed without much humor. "Believe me, I'm trying. Now that I've got the kids, I'm heading for the nearest international airport as fast as I can and getting the heck out of here."

"I'm glad."

Except he didn't sound glad at all. He sounded almost... bereft. "Are you going to miss me?" she breathed. She almost clapped a hand over her mouth, but the words were already out. When *was* she going to install a filter between her thoughts and her mouth?

He made eye contact with her, and what she saw in the depths of his gaze made her breath catch in her throat. He leaned forward slowly. "Yes, Elise," he murmured so softly she barely heard him. "I will miss you."

An urge to match his posture, to kiss him and make love to him roared through her. And yet, he refused to tell her who he was, refused to trust her, refused to let her into his life for real. He continued to hide behind his big bad arms dealer persona, even though it clearly wasn't who he really was. No man who rescued nuns and orphans was truly as violent and amoral as he claimed to be.

His voice low and charged, he asked, "Will you miss me?"

Instant answers leaped into her mind. Absolutely, she would miss him. Passionately. Desperately. Possibly, she'd miss him like that for the rest of her life. But for once, the words didn't cross her lips before she stopped to think. Did she dare give him that much power over her? He'd already made clear his willingness not to fight fair with her.

"I'm afraid," she whispered.

"Of me?" He froze, his mouth only a few inches from hers, alarm rising into his dark gaze.

"No. Of me."

His lips curved in a smile. "Aah, well. That's entirely different."

"Maybe for you," she retorted.

A silent laugh shook his shoulders. "Aah, my ever-feisty kitten. What am I going to do with you?"

She knew what she'd like him to do with her. But common sense warred with the desire coursing through her. She knew better. He was lying to her. He'd made it clear he planned to ditch her and the kids at the first opportunity. He was in some sort of violent business whether or not he was an arms dealer. She didn't even know if Drago was his real name. Somehow, she thought not.

But oh, how tempting he was. All that confidence and protectiveness and hidden decency. Not to mention all that lovely, lovely muscle—

No. She wasn't going to succumb to his charms, no matter how beautiful his smile or how sparkling and intelligent his eyes might be.

"I really shouldn't," he muttered.

"Shouldn't what?" she echoed in surprise.

"Shouldn't do this." He leaned forward the last few inches and kissed her. His mouth moved gently across hers, beguiling her even as it wiped away any words of protest she might have uttered. He was right. They shouldn't. But it felt oh so good.

"What's wrong with this, again?" she mumbled against his mouth.

His hand came up to cup the back of her head. "Nothing. Everything."

*Temptation.* That was the problem. Two weeks ago, she wouldn't have thought twice about jumping into the sack with him. But living as a nun, seeing the respect with which everyone treated her, having to resist worldly things—all of it had been a revelation. She did have the strength of will to pick and choose her mistakes. Furthermore, she had a responsibility to herself to do exactly that.

And logic told her sleeping with Drago Cantori would be a huge one.

Thing was, now that he knew she wasn't a nun, she didn't have that to hide behind as an excuse anymore. If she wanted him, she could have him. She snorted mentally. Wanting him wasn't any question. She wanted him more than anything she'd ever wanted in her life. The real question was, did she dare succumb to the attraction all but incinerating them both?

He nibbled lightly at her lips as if they had all the time in the world. Nearly groaning aloud with her need, she was acutely aware, however, that they might very well have only this one night. One shot at whatever it was simmering between them. She wouldn't go so far as to label it happiness. Sex with him would be spectacular, thrilling, perhaps even life changing. But she highly doubted at the end of the day she'd be happy she'd done it.

He'd go off into the jungle to play arms dealer, and she'd take the kids back to the real world and never see him again. The finality of it all struck her forcefully, and the loss was acutely painful. Except how could she lose what she'd never had?

And that brought her right back around to the core problem. Temptation. And its name was Drago Cantori.

"Kiss me, Elise. Let go just this once." As astute as always, he'd unerringly picked up on the source of her hesitation, darn him.

"But the children—"

He cut her off. "—Are asleep in the other room and Grandma's watching them."

That hadn't been where she was going. She'd meant to say her duty to them came first.

"They're fine. Don't be a coward and hide behind them."

A coward? She bristled inside. She was a lot of things, but a coward wasn't one of them. Except…maybe he was right. She'd spent so long seeking revenge for her parents' deaths that she'd closed out just about every other emotion but burning need for justice. The revelation broke over her like a cold shower: it wasn't the children or her nun disguise she'd been hiding behind. It was her parents and their tragic deaths. And she'd been hiding behind those for a very long time.

Five years she'd spent holding on to their murder. Five years living only for vengeance, seeking a way to make it right. Except there was no way to fix the fact that they were gone. Look at the damage her quest had done to Mia and Emanuel. How many more people was she going to hurt in her hopeless search for a way to make it better?

"Are you okay?" he asked, pulling back a little.

"Yes. No. Maybe."

"A quintessentially female answer if I ever heard one." He chuckled.

"It just dawned on me that I'm alive and my parents are dead, and all I can do is go on living. The one thing they'd never forgive me for would be stopping my life and dwelling forever on nothing but their murders."

"Am I supposed to have the slightest idea what you're talking about?"

She reached up to lay a hand on his cheek. "No. But thank you. I think I just figured out something important."

"All that from a kiss? Wait till you see the epiphany you get from making love with me."

She smiled, but maybe there was a kernel of truth in his words. Maybe she'd denied herself for too long. Shied away from truly living while she hid behind her grief and anger. And maybe that was why she threw her arms around his neck and, to his clear surprise, kissed him back.

This might be a guaranteed one-night stand, but that was a whole lot better than nothing at all. A sudden, driving need to connect to another human being, the tingle from head to foot with life, to feel something—anything—other than rage or guilt or grief overwhelmed her.

How did that saying go? *Carpe diem?* Seize the day. Truer words had never been spoken.

"Did you say something?" he muttered.

"I said *carpe diem*," she admitted in chagrin.

"No Latin, please." He chuckled. "You already caused me enough headaches when I thought I was in lust with a nun and going straight to hell for it."

Laughter bubbled up in her chest. "You have no idea how mad I was at Father Ambrose after I met you for sticking me in these hideous clothes and putting a wimple on my head."

"It really is an awful dress." His fingers drifted to the row of buttons down the front and commenced wiggling them free.

"Gee, thanks."

"Consider it a tribute to your beauty that I still thought you were hot in spite of it."

"Yeah, let's go with that." She laughed as he pushed the fabric off her shoulder and commenced sampling the valley just above her collarbone. But then the heat of his mouth closed on her breast through the skimpy lace of her not-at-all-nunlike bra and no more speech was possible for her.

She gasped and arched into him, and he absorbed her weight against him. She wrapped her arms around his head, drawing him even closer to her, dropping kisses on top of his head until he tilted his head back and captured her mouth with his.

Desire zinged through her body and she reveled in the sensation. She was alive. Really, truly alive!

Her clothes fell away like magic beneath his nimble fingers, and before long she straddled his hips completely naked against his fully clothed form. The rasp of his shirt was delicious and his hands were like hot branding irons, marking every inch of her flesh his.

"Better," he murmured against the cleft between her breasts.

"I'm feeling a little underdressed here," she announced breathlessly.

"I'd say you've got it just about right. I can't tell you how much I've wanted to get you out of those evil clothes. I've fantasized about it every night since I met you."

She smiled against his mouth. "Who knew the big, bad arms dealer was such a fashionista?"

He laughed and drew her closer, kissing her laughter into panting need. He was as thorough and leisurely a kisser as she'd expected, but frantic desire was singing through her veins, driving her mad. She didn't want leisurely right now.

Another night, she'd have reveled in the way his arms surrounded her in safety and how his body was solid and strong against hers. In another place, she'd love for a man like him to be her bulwark against the world forever. But tonight she didn't want safety. She wanted danger and lust and mind-blowing pleasure. All she had to do was reach out and take what he was offering. Her entire being sighed in relief as she gave up the last ghost of a fight against herself.

She pushed him down to the mattress and he fell backward, laughing. "Impatient, are you?"

"You have no idea. I've been waiting for this—for you—forever."

"I'm right here."

She pushed aside the thought that he didn't say he planned to stay with her. She was not going to wallow in wishes and regrets. She was going to enjoy this man, this moment, to the fullest. "I want it all, Drago. Promise me you won't hold anything back tonight."

His gaze met hers, abruptly serious, the intensity in it galvanizing. "Be careful what you wish for, little girl. You just might get it."

She stared back at him, matching every bit of his intensity. "Regardless of the wisdom of it, I know what I want."

"So be it." He twisted so she lay half beneath him, his body warm and protective over hers. She nearly sobbed in relief to feel the hard length of his arousal against her thigh.

She tugged at his shirt, and he lifted away enough for her to tug the cotton over his head and fling it aside. Acres of smooth skin and sculpted muscle unfolded before her. "Mmm. Yummy. Bring some of that on over here so I can have a taste."

And taste him she did. They took turns exploring each other's bodies with mouths and hands as she peeled off his trousers and briefs and finally laid him as bare as her. She wasn't exactly sure when she made the decision that this was what she wanted. But now that it was made, she was absolutely certain she didn't want to turn back. Tomorrow would be soon enough for the regrets.

True to his word, Drago held nothing back, showed her no mercy, gave her nowhere to hide. It all became a tangle of sheets and pillows and hot flesh and heavy breathing. Before long she lost track of where she ended and he began. He seemed to take pleasure in making her cry out with need and pushed her harder and harder until she thrashed mindlessly beneath him, surging against him again and again.

Everything beyond the two of them ceased to exist. It was just him and her and the pleasure rumbling like a rocket engine on a launchpad between them, rattling harder and harder as the power built, waiting to explode. Steam heat rolled forth. Sparks and geysers of flame shot between them, and the bed shook as their climax lifted off between them. It gathered speed and power as it roared into space, dragging them along with it, so brilliant she had to squint against its glory.

And when the void would have claimed her, Drago was there, his face filling her field of view, his gaze boring into her, stripping her bare even as his smile filled her with joy. Completion. Rightness.

She fell back to the damp sheets gasping. The two of them were meant to be. No matter if he dealt in death for a living. No matter if his work was ridiculously dangerous. No matter that loving him could only lead to loss and grief. It was a done deal.

"Who are you?" she whispered.

He smiled disarmingly. "I'm the guy you just took to the moon."

He'd evaded her yet again. Even now. Even in this most intimate of moments, he'd dodged the truth. The sad part was she loved him anyway, wanted him anyway. She shouldn't forgive him for it, but God help her, she did.

# Chapter 11

Ted's arm was asleep, but Elise was lying on it, and he wouldn't disturb her right now for anything in the world. Who'd have guessed all that fire was hiding beneath her demure exterior? She wasn't a kitten. She was a wildcat. He caught himself smiling up at the ceiling in the dark and started. Since when did a roll in the sack make him this giddy with joy?

Since he'd met Elise, apparently. And that was a problem. He was supposed to be quelling a dangerous terrorist plot and not skipping through the daisies with some do-gooder, fake nun. But as sure as she was lying beside him, he was on the verge of breaking out in tra-la-las and kumbayas.

He had to get his head back in the game. He had to make contact with the real leader of the Army of Freedom. Figure out if he was being played. If they'd penetrated his disguise. If they actually planned to attack a bunch of civilian airliners on American soil. And if it came down to it, he might have to mark this Eduardo Lentano guy and his key cadre for execution.

Although, the idea left a bad taste in his mouth. Images of Mia and Emanuel's too-serious eyes flashed through his head. How many more orphans would he create if he wiped out Lentano and his men?

Irritated, he asked himself fiercely how many American orphans would be created if he let these guys blow up a bunch of airplanes. Violence left behind innocent victims either way. The only question was whether they were your victims or the other guy's. Personally, he opted for the other guy's. Especially if the other guy picked the fight in the first place. Although, he supposed that point could be debated, too.

Since when did he question his work like this? He'd wrestled through these moral questions years ago and never looked back. Somebody had to do his job. Better that a moral guy like him who wouldn't get lost in it should do the job than some schmuck who'd go psycho eventually. But the argument rang hollow with him, tonight.

For the first time, the violent nature of his work left a sour taste in his mouth. Seeing himself through Elise's eyes wasn't a pleasant thing. He wanted her to see a hero when she looked at him. He didn't want to be the cold-blooded killer she accused him of being.

Maybe his loss of detachment was a warning sign he'd be wise to heed. Being able to remove himself emotionally from the situation at hand was vital to his work. Men like him learned to cut off all their feelings—fear, anger, guilt—and to focus purely on doing the mission. It was one of the great secrets to success of special operators.

But then along came a spitfire in a wimple with sparkling eyes and sweet curves and a smile that made him feel a mile tall. What had she *done* to him? Whatever the hell it was, he had to undo it, and fast. He reached for his usual chilly calm…and got nothing. Zilch. As he looked inside himself, all he saw was a raging need to roll over and make love to Elise again.

Talk about screwed. Man, this was it. Every fiber of his being shouted for him to collect the kids and Grandma and Elise and get the heck out of this country. But that was the one thing he couldn't do. Not yet. First, he had a mission to complete. And then…

…and then he'd be back to collect his little brood. A brood he'd come to care for more deeply than he could ever have imagined.

With that in mind, he carefully slipped out from under Elise and dressed silently. He eased the door open and slipped out into the hall. He was done waiting for the Army of Freedom to come to him. It was time to take the mission directly to the enemy.

Elise opened her eyes as Drago slipped out of the room. Where was he going? Back to his room? Or someplace else? Someplace where she wouldn't find him? Was he ditching her as she'd feared he would?

She'd thought their lovemaking had been pretty incredible, the connection between them powerful and real. But had it been nothing special to him, after all? Or did she have it all wrong? Was he heading out to find the rebels by himself? It would be his style. Protect the women and children by being the big, macho man all by himself.

She slipped out from under the covers and pulled on her hated nun's garb. It felt even weirder than usual to don it after what she'd spent most of the night doing. What a fraud she was. She'd spent so much of the past few years hiding that she'd forgotten how to be herself. But thanks to Drago, it had all come back to her—the joy, the terror, the vulnerability, the passion of it all. Being alive again was a wonderful thing.

And with that in mind, she wasn't about to let him charge out into the jungle and get himself killed, thank you very much.

She hurried down the hall frantically trying to figure out how she was going to follow Drago if he left the hotel in the Jeep. Maybe she could convince the hotel clerk to let her borrow his vehicle. But that would take time. She put on an extra burst of speed and reached the lobby just as Drago was leaving, his tall silhouette unmistakable.

She ran to the front doors and was abjectly relieved to see him closing the back door of the Jeep. Apparently, he'd just been getting something out of the back of it. He moved past the parking lot and headed out on foot into the town, striding confidently down the street as though he knew where he was going. How was that? Memory of him making that phone call to get directions to Mercado flashed into her mind.

He'd lied to her. He wasn't entirely without backup out here. Someone was helping him. She turned onto the side street he'd disappeared down a minute ago and lengthened her stride to keep pace with him far ahead. What else had he lied to her about?

Or maybe the real question was, what hadn't he lied to her about? Was Drago Cantori even his name? Was he from France? Did he really love her?

Her thoughts screeched to a halt. Had everything about their lovemaking been a lie, too? He hadn't talked a lot, but she'd thought he'd been making silent promises to her with his body and soul. Maybe he hadn't promised her till death do they part, but he'd seemed to imply that he wanted a lot more of her and was prepared to pursue a relationship of some kind with her. Or had that been merely wishful thinking on her part?

She was so nailing him down and having a serious talk with him when she caught up with him. One thing she knew for sure. If the two of them were going to have a real relationship, he'd have to come clean and be honest with her.

But as soon as the wave of indignation at him passed, desperate longing for him under any circumstances—honesty or no—came roaring back to the fore. Sheesh. She was a mess! She knew better than to stand for a man who wouldn't be square with her. But memory of their love-making rolled over her, making her knees weak and her gaze limpid as she peered ahead in the dark at his fast-moving form.

Aah, temptation, thy name is Drago.

He stopped abruptly ahead of her, forcing her to duck into a doorway in case he happened to glance back over his shoulder. After a moment, she peeked around the corner. He was doing the same, plastered against a wall ahead and looking carefully at something down a side street.

He must have found the Devil's Den Hotel. Fear for him exploded in her gut along with a driving need to protect her man. As he slipped around the corner and disappeared from sight, she sprinted forward and took his place against the wall. Mimicking his actions, she peeked around the corner.

The street was quiet and unnaturally dark. All the street-lights were out, or more likely intentionally out of commission. She was just in time to see the front door of a three-story building close. She couldn't see a sign from here, but she'd bet her life savings that was the Devil's Den.

Now what was she supposed to do? Drago had an

excuse to just barge in. He could sell them some machine guns or something. But she couldn't exactly charge in and offer to cook for everyone or hear confessions. Maybe she could sneak in the back door and hear something. Although, if it really was the Army of Freedom headquarters, all the entrances were likely guarded. She didn't see anyone out in this street, though. She peeked again, taking her time to search for lookouts. If they were there, they were very well hidden.

Instead of following Drago, she retraced her steps to the next side street and circled around the block to approach the hotel from the other side. She didn't see anyone from this angle, either. Cautiously, she slipped into the alley beside the hotel. She looked for surveillance cameras or bums apparently asleep that the gangs in New York used around their hangouts. Nothing. Surely the Army of Freedom wasn't so confident it didn't bother with such things. The Colombian Army was no slouch when it came to equipment and training.

She touched the white-edged black cloth over her hair self-consciously. Just how much protection would it provide her when push came to shove? If nothing else, Grandma knew Father Ambrose's name, and the priest's phone number was in the woman's cell phone now. If Elise died out of sheer stupidity tonight, Grandma could call the padre and get help pulling the children out of harm's way.

For sure, following Drago was stupid with a capital S. But she could no more turn away from him than she could the children. Where she loved, she protected. It was just the way she was wired. Although, how she was going to help him in any way, she hadn't the slightest idea.

A door came into sight on her right. A peek in through the dirty window revealed a commercial kitchen. She tried the knob. Locked. Of course. Too bad one of her regular patients was an accomplished lock picker and had shown her a trick or two. A credit card really did work if the lock was simple and a person had a little patience and luck. She left it in God's hands. If she managed to open the door, clearly she was meant to go inside.

It took a few minutes, but the door cracked open under her hands. *Okay, God. Here goes nothing.*

There was nothing like a bold approach to disarm the enemy. Of course, it was also the fastest way to take a spray of bullets in the chest if it failed. Ted walked right into the middle of the dim lobby and announced to no one in particular, "My name is Drago Cantori, and I'm here to see Eduardo Lentano."

And then he waited. He imagined several sleepy men somewhere in the hotel were scrambling hard, trying to figure out what to do about him. When no one came out to meet him, he moved over to an armchair and sat down, sprawling comfortably as if he didn't have a care in the world.

It took nearly ten minutes, but finally, a grim-looking fellow who could use a shave stepped out from behind the front counter.

"Mr. Cantori. To what do we owe this pleasure?"

"I'm here to finish my deal with the Army of Freedom. I'm tired of playing along with your little games. Let's either cut to the chase and close this thing, or I walk." He shrugged to indicate that he didn't care particularly which happened.

"People don't just walk out of this place, Mr. Cantori."

Ted grinned, belying the menace of his response. "I do."

"How's that?"

Ted ignored the question and instead examined his fingernails one by one. No way was he showing his hand to some flunky.

A growl rumbled in the man's chest before he turned and stormed over to the elevator and punched a button angrily. The elevator came and left.

Ted looked at his watch. Thirty-seven seconds until the elevator door opened again and another man stepped out. He tsked at the next man up the ladder of command. "I'd watch that guy's temper if I were you. His self-control is dismal."

This guy pursed his lips in apparent amusement, but his eyes were cold and hard. "What brings you to this place at such a late hour, Mr. Cantori?"

Ted waved a casual hand. "My line of work has no regular hours. Business before sleep, I say."

The other man didn't seem impressed. "Who is this Eduardo Lentano you say you wish to speak with?"

Ted stood and took a step toward the front door, indicating his intention to leave. He pitched his voice in tones so gentle that Lentano's man would cringe in fear if he knew what was good for him. "Don't jack me around, amigo. You think a man like me doesn't do my homework? I'm not some amateur you can lead around by the nose. I was willing to play along for a little while, but I've run out of patience."

Lentano's lieutenant snorted. "From where I stand, you're worse than an amateur. What arms dealer collects nuns and children and hauls them around with him? They slow you down. Make you vulnerable. They make you soft."

Ted's heart skipped a beat. These guys knew about Elise and the kids? How badly had he underestimated this bunch? And how much danger were Elise and the children in? An urge to turn around and run back to them nearly overwhelmed him. Shocked, he stilled the urge. How badly had his brood of misfits gotten under his skin, anyway? Indeed, he was every bit as vulnerable as the man before him said. But at all costs, he couldn't let on to it.

Ted laughed in what he hoped was a convincing manner. "Then they worked, the women and children. If you think I'm not dangerous or effective, then so does the Colombian Army. Haven't you ever heard of establishing a cover, my friend?"

The man stared skeptically. "A nun? An old lady? Little children?"

"I'm here, aren't I?"

Would the rebels believe his lie that she and the kids had been merely a cover? It was a flimsy story at best. And her life, Grandma's and the children's, might very well depend on it. She shifted slightly in an effort to see the rebel's face, her thighs screaming in protest at her awkward position under a table inside the dark, empty restaurant. All she saw were men coming into the lobby carrying guns of all shapes and sizes.

She ought to turn around and leave this very second. She'd head back to the hotel, collect Grandma and the kids, steal his Jeep and leave this place. But there were enough men out there now that she was terrified someone would spot the kitchen door opening if she tried to slip out.

She couldn't believe Drago had dragged them into something this dangerous. Her heart screamed in betrayal that he would risk their lives like this, but her mind dropped firmly into denial. Surely, he wouldn't intentionally endanger her. She'd been there when they made love, had looked into his eyes. Nobody was that good a liar, were they? Although, Lord knew, he'd lied to her constantly pretty much from day one. Heck, she was sure she didn't even know his real name.

The man in the lobby was talking to Drago again. "…need you to have a seat."

She frowned. What was up with that silky tone of voice? That sounded almost like a threat.

Drago took his time perching on the arm of the chair he'd been sitting in before. Not quite outright defiance, but enough to let Lentano's man know he wasn't cowed.

"You will have to wait for the others to join us. It is very late."

"Or very early," Drago replied. "It's all a matter of perspective, isn't it?"

He pulled out his cell phone and casually typed out a text message, almost as if defying the Army of Freedom man to stop him. Elise wondered who Drago was contacting and what he was saying. Maybe he was finally calling in some backup. She *hoped* that was what he was doing. He was alone—well, almost alone. She wasn't exactly the cavalry—and he was firmly in enemy territory. Worse, the enemy seemed none too pleased to have him there.

If nothing else, sending a text message like that had to make the Army of Freedom people at least wonder if he did have armed support nearby. Yet again, she was impressed by Drago's ability to handle himself in a tight situation. Very carefully, she eased into a more comfortable position to wait out the delay while Lentano and company woke up, got up, got dressed and came down to talk to Drago.

While she waited, she inched the tablecloth down and to the right to better cover her from the view of anyone in the lobby, or from the kitchen. Anyone passing through here casually shouldn't spot her.

Perhaps another ten minutes passed in silence, Drago

texting sporadically with someone, and Lentano's man scowling ever more darkly as the text conversation continued.

Finally, the lieutenant couldn't stand it any longer and blurted, "Who are you communicating with?"

Drago answered lightly, "One of my big clients."

Elise grinned. The implication was clear: the Army of Freedom was small potatoes in his world. Perhaps the lieutenant would have made a snarky remark in return, but just then the elevator door opened and a dozen men streamed into the lobby. Her breath caught. They were big, mean-looking and armed to the last man if the bulges under their jackets were any indication.

Drago studied the group for a moment and then unerringly stepped toward one of the men standing inconspicuously to one side. "Eduardo Lentano. Finally, we meet."

The man frowned. "How did you know which one I was?"

"My business requires me to read people." He added gently, "I'm very good at my job."

"Good? You have no references. You have no reputation. You come into my territory and claim to be some big badass weapons broker. Why should I do business with you?"

Drago's stance was relaxed…almost too relaxed. He looked ready to erupt into violence at the first provocation. "If you can find nothing on me, that means I'm very, very good at my job. Did you seriously expect me to blow into Colombia and show a high profile to the government? To make a target of myself in order to impress the likes of you? That's not how real arms dealers do business, Mr. Lentano."

The insurgent leader looked stung. Furious, even.

"Was your man Raoul speaking truthfully when he expressed an interest in purchasing surface-to-air missiles?"

Lentano's eyes lit with unholy greed and Elise's jaw dropped. Drago was going to sell this maniac *missiles?*

Drago continued. "Let me guess where you want them delivered. New York City. Washington, D.C. Los Angeles, maybe? And you need them big enough to take out an airliner, yes?"

"Can you do it?" Lentano snapped.

Mother of God. This guy was planning a terrorist attack on the United States. Drago was nodding slowly, more as if in satisfaction that he'd guessed right than as if giving an affirmative answer to Lentano.

"Before we talk money, Cantori, tell me something. Why do you run around with women and children like a one-man charity?"

Drago shrugged at the rebel leader's question. "We already went over that. They were a cover. An excuse for my heading into this area."

The Army of Freedom leader grinned broadly, as though Drago had just said exactly what the guy wanted him to say. Like Drago had just walked into a trap. The Colombian asked archly, "Then you won't mind eliminating them?"

"Eliminating the women and children? Why bother?" Drago shrugged.

Well, that was good news, at least. He wasn't leaping all over the idea of killing her and the kids.

The front door to the lobby opened, and a half dozen men strode into the open space. Elise gasped and had to throw a hand over her mouth at the sight of Mia, Emanuel, and Grandma, bleary-eyed and terrified in the middle of the cluster of armed insurgents.

"Kill them, Drago Cantori. Prove to me you're who you say you are."

"How does killing an old lady and a couple of kids prove that? I could be any psychopath running around in the jungle and do that." Drago added scornfully, "I am a businessman, not a murderer."

Lentano shrugged. "Fine. Then I will kill them."

Elise's horrified gaze locked on Drago. *Do something!* she shouted at him in her mind. But he merely pulled out his cell phone and sent yet another completely infuriating text message. He pocketed the phone unhurriedly.

"I wouldn't do that if I were you," he commented.

"Why not?"

"Much bigger fish in the sea than you are interested in those kids. Kill them, and you and your little Army of Freedom fighters will be wiped off the face of the earth."

The insurgents froze, the vignette taking on a surreal quality. She could not believe he'd give up two innocent children like that! Hatred blossomed in her soul, but she shoved it down brutally. She had no time for that. Right now she had to figure out a way to save Mia and Emanuel. But how on earth was she supposed to take on twenty armed men by herself? She was one woman. Unarmed. Untrained for this sort of thing.

She was also the only hope Mia and Emanuel had left. At a complete and desperate loss, she squeezed her eyes shut and prayed for a miracle.

## Chapter 12

Ted had been in some bad situations in his life, but this took the cake, hands down. Three hostages was bad enough, but the odds were twenty to one against him. Half that many hostiles he could've handled, but the sheer number of rebels around him would do him in.

Lentano spoke almost jovially. "There's only one little problem, my friend. I think you're a fake. You talk a good line, have a slick answer for every question I ask. But I don't think you are who you say you are. You planning to steal my money and disappear, maybe?" His voice rose on a note of anger and the smiled faded from his face. "You think I'm stupid?"

Ted knew exactly how this scenario went. The guy would work himself up into a frenzy and order his men to open fire.

However, he'd spent the past half hour preparing for just that eventuality. He'd arranged a surprise for Lentano and his Army of Freedom. A little something to even up the odds if it came to a firefight. He spoke aloud, knowing the gang at H.O.T. Watch would be listening to the microphone sewn into his collar and knowing they would understand he was actually talking to them. "You guys ready?"

Lentano looked at him as though he'd lost his mind. "For what?"

As Ted spoke, the smile faded from his face until nothing but death radiated from him. "For a small demonstration of why it's very, very bad form to insult a man like me."

The hotel's front door cracked open. Everyone spun to face it, yanking out pistols and pointing them at the empty doorway. A squat silver box about two feet tall and wide and maybe three feet long rolled into the lobby.

Lentano began to laugh. "What the hell is that?"

Ted answered, "That is known in the business as Robo-SEAL. Perhaps a small demonstration of its capability would be in order."

A half dozen doors flipped open without warning and all of a sudden, the box was bristling with gun barrels. The insurgents turned their weapons on the box threateningly. He wondered if they had any idea how silly they looked drawing on a squat little robot. Of course, they didn't know that RoboSEAL was armored with high-tech alloys and being operated by an entire team of remote warfare technicians at H.O.T. Watch headquarters. It had been designed to withstand better than the likes of them.

Drago dove for Mia and Emanuel, who were on the other side of a sofa from him. Grabbing one in each arm, he rolled to the floor as RoboSEAL opened fire. He could only hope that Grandma had the sense to duck and follow him to cover. Thankfully, she did.

Mia screamed against his chest, and he held her tight as

a deafening explosion of noise and muzzle flashes erupted. He was traumatizing an already traumatized child, but what choice did he have? He couldn't let Lentano kill her.

He shoved the children at Grandma and pulled out his own weapons as he sprinted across an open space to take cover behind a pillar well away from the three of them. He needed to draw the fire in his direction once Lentano's men realized they were having no effect on RoboSEAL.

Men had scattered in all directions and six were already down in pools of their own blood. The robot was rolling forward, continuing to spray lead in deadly bursts. Another man went down before Ted dived for cover.

"Get Cantori!" Lentano screamed.

Chips of concrete flew past his face as at least several of the insurgents turned their fire on him. Crouching low, Ted spun out from behind the pillar and took two quick shots. Another man down.

A voice in his ear complained, "Tell us the next time you break cover, Captain, and we'll lay down covering fire for you."

"Roger," he bit out. "Now." He spun out again as RoboSEAL erupted in flashes of light and sound. Ted took out two more men before he had to jump back behind the pillar. A sharp pain in his side announced that his bullet-resistant vest had taken a hit.

He took an experimental deep breath. No problem. He wasn't injured. By his count, it was down to about ten men out there now. That was the good news. The bad news was the surviving rebels had all found cover of their own. And Grandma and the kids were still pinned down behind that couch out in the middle of the room. As soon as one of the rebels got over his shock long enough to engage his brain, one of them would turn his weapon on the helpless old woman and children.

He slammed new clips into both of his pistols, wielding one in each hand. He announced to H.O.T. Watch, "I've got to get the kids. Give me cover."

"Negative. Too many targets," someone from H.O.T. Watch retorted.

"Too bad. I gotta go."

"Don't be a—"

Whether the voice would've called him a hero or an idiot, Ted never found out because he charged out from behind the pillar, shooting simultaneously with both hands. His accuracy dropped considerably when he had to fire like this, and he went through ammunition like crazy, but the shock value was high. More to the point, the bad guys all ducked for cover.

Time slowed to a crawl as he ran. Insurgents locked onto him with eyes and weapons in slow motion as he ran across their fields of fire. And then a tremendous explosion erupted behind him, knocking him off his feet and rendering him partially deaf. His ears rung and white lights danced in front of his eyes as he rolled onto his back.

Holy Mother of God.

Elise. And she looked like an avenging angel, with a second Molotov cocktail at the ready in her right hand. A huge fireball rose up in front of Eduardo Lentano, as whatever flammable substance she'd filled the bottle with burned furiously.

As he finished the roll and came to his knees, she threw the second Molotov cocktail. The men between Ted and the children threw up their arms protectively and fell back from the exploding flames.

It was just the opening he needed. Ted raced to the sofa. Emanuel cowered in Grandma's arms, and Ted scooped up Mia. "This way!" he shouted over the roaring fires, the shooting robot, the screams of the dying and the chaos of Lentano trying to rally his men.

For a seventy-year-old, Grandma was pretty spry. Or maybe it had something to do with the roomful of flying lead, but the woman stayed right at Ted's side as he sprinted for the front door. He barreled through it with Grandma on his heels. He shoved Mia at Grandma with a single terse instruction. "Run!"

He had to go back for Elise.

"Cover the front door with RoboSEAL," he ordered as he spun back into hell. "Don't let *anyone* exit this way."

The robot was laying waste to the hotel lobby as he charged back inside. Lentano was down in a massive pool of blood that announced the man's death. His remaining lieutenants were panicked, firing wildly at anything and anyone. If they weren't careful, they'd be shooting each other soon.

"Get out of there!" someone shouted in his earpiece.

He ignored the command. Elise was not in sight. The last time he'd glimpsed her, she'd been standing in the doorway of the kitchen. On the assumption that she'd retreated there, he raced through the little restaurant and headed for the swinging doors.

He spun into the kitchen and dodged hard as something shiny and sharp spun past his head, barely missing him. A butcher knife clattered to the floor.

"It's me!" he called out as another knife came winging his way.

Elise stood up behind a preparation counter. "What are you doing here?"

"Rescuing you," he snapped. "If you'll quit throwing knives at me." He looked around fast and spotted a tower for stacking dirty dishes. He rolled it beside the doorway and knocked it over on its side. It wouldn't stop the doors from opening, but it might trip someone running through.

"How did you get in here?" he demanded.

"There's a back door," she panted.

"Show me."

He followed her lithe form as she twisted through the dark kitchen. Her eyes were much better adapted to the dark than his were at the moment. He banged his head against a hanging pan and it clanged noisily. He swore aloud.

Sure enough, H.O.T. Watch announced, "You're about to have company."

"I'm way low on ammo," he reported. He needed to improvise. And fast. He threw open the big commercial ovens and was intensely relieved to see they were gas fueled. Perfect.

Spying a ball of cooking twine, he snatched that up and rolled a tower holding trays of clean glasses forward next to the aisle. A couple quick loops of twine around the prep table leg and the top of the tower, and someone was in for a nasty surprise. Broken glass would go everywhere when someone tripped over that twine.

Scooping up a half dozen knives, he joined her where she crouched by the service exit.

"Let's go," she whispered urgently, reaching for the door handle.

"Wait," he bit out.

She threw him a questioning look.

"Lentano's guys will cover the alley."

She frowned then muttered, "Do you smell gas?"

"I darn well hope so. I've got all the stoves turned on full blast."

"Why?"

"Plan B." He got no time to elaborate, though, because

the restaurant doors rattled. "Showtime," he murmured into his collar.

"Five hostiles massed outside the kitchen," someone announced in his ear. "Heavily armed but not setting up to quarter the kitchen."

Not professionals, then.

He whispered to Elise, "Waistband of my pants. Take the pistol. Nine shots in the clip, one in the chamber." He felt her hand move against his back. It was his emergency backup weapon, but he'd rather she have it than him.

The double doors crashed open and several men charged forward. Two of them went sprawling over the overturned cart and the others jumped awkwardly. He popped up and winged a carving knife at the confused men. Someone cried out as he launched the second blade. Another shout. Ricochets pinged all around Ted and Elise, and he threw an arm over her shoulders and shoved her down to the floor.

"When I say to, pop up and fire like mad," he whispered in her ear.

Lentano's men shouted and raced forward.

"Now!" Ted shouted as he fired both his pistols.

A tremendous crash of glass breaking intruded upon the firefight. Men swore and jumped in all directions as shards of glass flew. In the chaos, Ted took out two more men with careful shots to the head. Gut shots were easier targets, but a single head shot would stop most men. And by his count he only had a few bullets left.

He slammed in his last clip and gestured at Elise to cease fire. The kitchen went quiet. Lentano's men retreated to huddle by the kitchen door.

"What are they waiting for?" Elise breathed. "We're almost out of ammunition."

"They don't know that." After a murmured conversation, most of the men left the kitchen at a run. "They're coming around to the back door," he whispered. He smiled as RoboSEAL cut loose in the lobby. Things might not be great in here, but Lentano's men weren't having a picnic tonight, either.

"We need to *go*," Elise muttered from between clenched teeth.

She sounded close to panic. Which he supposed was a logical reaction to the situation. But he wasn't quite done with Lentano's men. "Not yet."

Thankfully, she seemed to trust him and stayed put.

The gas smell was almost strong enough, but not quite. He gave it a few more seconds and then gestured toward the back door at Elise. She crawled the few feet to it and reached for the handle. He shouted at her to go as at the same time he fired his last few rounds at the stoves.

The ovens made a whooshing sound first, and then great balls of fire rolled out as the gas fumes detonated. Ted dived after Elise, landing beside her as a concussion of searing heat slammed into his back. He leaped to his feet, hauled her up and snatched the pistol she held out to him.

He took the gun and grabbed her hand as they took off running. Two men popped up in front of them, and on the run, he double-tapped shots at both men. They were hard shots and, although he hit both men, only one dropped. The other staggered but raised a weapon as Ted and Elise closed in on him.

At this range, the man stood a good chance of hitting and possibly killing them. Panic for Elise's safety roared through him. Ted took a flying leap at the other man and slammed into the guy just as the man's gun fired.

Something hot and hard slammed into his left shoulder as he impacted the man. He grabbed the man's chin and yanked hard to the right. A sickening crunch accompanied the man's broken neck. The guy dropped like a stone and Ted collapsed on top of him.

"Are you hit?" Elise's hands were on him as he rolled over onto his back.

"Shoulder."

She pressed her palm against the joint, but he shook her off. "I have to stop the bleeding," she protested.

"Later," he snapped.

"If you're losing enough blood, there won't be a later," she snapped back.

As he climbed painfully to his feet, he ground out, "If we don't move, you'll die."

"Tough. I'm not letting you bleed to death."

He scooped up the fallen man's semiautomatic weapon. It felt heavy, as though it was fully loaded. Praise the Lord. A pair of men rounded the corner into the alley and he fired from the waist, dropping both men efficiently. But hot pokers of agony exploded in his shoulder. The joint was hit. As soon as his adrenaline rush wore off, he would lose use of the limb.

Thankfully, his legs worked and he sprinted for the mouth of the alley. As he passed the two downed men, he paused long enough to pick up their weapons, as well. He passed a shotgun to Elise and shouldered the sling on the automatic machine pistol.

Several shadows rounded the corner and he spun behind the lone Dumpster. Elise had the good sense to mimic him.

"We're pinned down," she whispered frantically.

"Not hardly. Just do it like we did it in the jungle," he instructed her. With as much ammunition as he had now, he wasn't the slightest bit worried about the men in front of him. He popped to fire above the Dumpster, then spun out from beside it to fire again. He wasn't one of the top marksmen in the U.S. military for nothing. In under a minute, the alley was littered with bodies and no one stood between them and freedom.

He moved out from behind the Dumpster in a half crouch, weapon at the ready. His shoulder was starting to lock up, and the pain was incredible. Only knowledge that Elise's life rode on him getting her out of here kept him from crumpling to the ground.

He reached the corner and crouched, peeking around the corner quickly and then ducking back. The street he'd glimpsed was clear. Lentano and his men probably didn't know what had hit them. What with RoboSEAL going crazy and him doing the whole killing machine thing, the Army of Freedom was down a whole lot of men at the moment.

Finally, he heard the sirens he'd been waiting for.

"Let's move out," he murmured to Elise over his shoulder.

He stood upright and moved out of the alley, walking rapidly down the street. He cleared every doorway aggressively, weapon first. But with each abrupt turn, his shoulder throbbed a little worse, the ice picks of agony shooting a little farther down his arm and across his chest. He had a matter of minutes of useful function left, and then he was finished.

They moved about three blocks from the hotel before he finally turned into the darkest alley he could find.

"I'm done," he gasped as he slid down the wall.

"Idiot," Elise whispered angrily as she squatted beside him. She efficiently tore his shirt clear of his shoulder and reached behind him to check for an exit wound. "The bullet's still in there. You need surgery to remove it and stop the bleeding, not to mention to repair the joint."

"You offering to do all that?" he gritted out.

She snorted and didn't bother to answer. "Lean forward so I can take off your shirt."

He complied with a groan. She was relieved to see he was wearing a bulletproof vest, but then spotted at least four big splats on the mesh fabric where bullets had impacted it. Shuddering at how close he'd come to dying more than once already, she tore off a strip from the bottom of the shirt, then wadded up the rest of it and jammed it against the entry wound. Her face spun and lights danced in his eyes as the worst pain he'd ever experienced ripped through him.

"Stay with me," she bit out as she bound the impromptu bandage in place. "You're too big for me to move if you pass out."

He fought to hang on to consciousness and managed to pant, "Talk to me."

She nodded. "You're bleeding badly, but haven't lost enough blood to die, yet. I've seen worse, but we need to get you medical care ASAP. Can you walk?"

"Don't know."

"Well, give it a try." She hoisted him under his good shoulder, and with her help he managed to haul himself to his feet. He swayed violently.

"Lean against the wall for a minute until you get your balance."

Finally, the world stopped spinning too badly and he nodded at her.

"Okay. Let's go, Rambo. Where do you suppose the nearest hospital is?"

"No hospital," he rasped.

She stared up at him in disbelief. "You need a hospital. You may die if you don't get that treated."

"You do it."

"I'm not qualified to deal with that. You've been shot."

He unclenched his teeth enough to mumble, "You've seen gunshots in New York, I bet."

"This is a bad one, Drago. You need a pro."

He shook his head resolutely.

"I'm not arguing with you," she announced.

"Good." He took a step and then stopped. "Gun."

She frowned, then looked around on the ground. Impatiently, she picked up the weapon he'd stolen and flung the strap over her shoulder. "Where to?"

"Hotel."

"I'm not going back there!" she exclaimed.

"We need wheels."

"Oh. Of course. The Jeep. Then I can drive you to a hospital. Good idea."

He didn't argue with her. They did need to get to the Jeep, or more precisely, her medical kit in the back of it. No way was he going to a hospital. He'd be thrown in jail the minute he showed his face. But he'd fight that fight with her if he made it back to their hotel alive.

Two police cars appeared on the street ahead and he nearly passed out when he and Elise jumped into a recessed doorway to avoid the approaching headlights. The cars sped past, sirens blaring.

"Where are Mia and Emanuel?" she murmured as they moved out again.

"With Grandma. I told her to run."

"Thank God they all made it out of the hotel."

He merely grunted in response.

The citizens of Mercado, no strangers to gun battles, apparently, were staying completely off the streets. The rest of their walk back to the hotel was undisturbed. Which was a good thing. He was hanging on to consciousness by a thread. Only Elise's steady stream of salty commentary on the stupidity of heroes kept him going.

Finally the hotel came into view. One more block to go. He staggered and nearly went down. Elise jumped and managed to get her shoulder under his right arm before he fell. "Only a little bit more," she encouraged him. "You're doing great."

One thing he knew for sure about nurses. If they said you were doing great in that particular tone of voice, you were about three quarters of the way to dead.

"Jeep," he gasped.

"Right." She veered into the parking lot and guided him to the Jeep.

"Key. Right front pocket."

She propped him against the vehicle and dug into his pocket. "Got it."

She made as if to put him in the passenger seat, but he shook his head. "Your med kit. In the back."

"I'm serious, Drago. You need a hospital."

He mumbled, "Government will arrest me."

She stared at him in dismay. "*Now* you tell me this?"

"Get your kit," he gasped.

"Don't you faint on me. I'm not doing surgery on you in some parking lot," she threatened.

Not good. Nurses only threatened when you were about to die. Reaching for the last dregs of strength he could muster, he staggered to the hotel door. He made it to the elevator, but his legs collapsed as it lurched into motion.

"Don't you dare give up on me, Drago Cantori," Elise ground out. "Get up." When he didn't move, she said more forcefully, "Get up!"

It was so hard to follow her order. He was slipping into a warm, comfortable place where the pain was receding and panic had no meaning. Something impacted his cheek sharp and hard. Did she just *slap* him? Vague indignation pushed back the beckoning blanket of white just a little.

"Walk, buster."

Someone dragged insistently at his right arm and he didn't have the energy to fight it. He stumbled forward. A door loomed and then opened. He was pulled forward into a room. A bed rose before him. At long last. He smiled at the sight of it and gave up the fight.

Elise gasped as Drago passed out on the bed. She'd expected it, but it was still alarming to see such a strong, invincible guy go down like that. At least he was unconscious. She dumped the contents of the med kit on the mattress beside Drago and frantically went to work. She peeled off the Kevlar vest and cut away the makeshift bandage. A new flow of blood gushed over his shoulder.

She grabbed a scalpel and sliced the wound further open. She spotted the big bleeder right away and clamped it so she could go hunting for the bullet. She found the mashed bit of metal lodged up against his rotator cuff, which was shredded. She winced at the damage. Even with good reconstructive surgery, the joint was done for.

The bullet was slippery and she finally had to wedge her fingernail under the damned thing to get it out. She didn't have the supplies to irrigate the wound and properly clean it and could only pour hydrogen peroxide into the area and hope it was enough.

The peroxide flushed the wound a bit and she spotted two smaller bleeders, which she used her last clamp to close off together. It was meatball surgery at its worst. She could only pray he stayed unconscious until she was done. She wasn't strong enough to hold him down if he started to thrash around.

She used a lighter to heat up the scalpel as much as she could and cauterized the two small bleeding veins. The smell of burning flesh made her nauseous, but she pressed on grimly. If Drago could win a firefight and walk back to the hotel with this, she could at least fix his wound.

The big vein would have to be stitched and cauterized or else he'd bleed to death. Grimacing, she did what she had to do. Another liberal splash of peroxide in the wound and it was time to close up. She stitched the deep tissue as best she could, but she was no orthopedic surgeon. She did her best to connect the right muscle tissue bits together, but who knew if he'd be able to use the joint again after this.

She closed the mouth of the wound as best she could, but the ragged result was going to leave a nasty scar. One final dousing with the last of the peroxide, and she was ready to bandage up the wound.

Now to wake up Drago and keep him from going into worse shock than he was already in. She fished out all the little cans of orange juice from the room's mini-fridge and carried them over to the bed.

"Wake up, Drago," she called. She slapped him lightly, then more forcefully.

His eyelids fluttered but did not open.

"Don't make me hit you again," she threatened.

One eye peeled open a bit. "Will hit. Back," he mumbled.

Thank God. He was lucid, if groggy. "Drink this." She lifted his head and poured orange juice down his throat. He coughed and sputtered, but seemed to regain a little more consciousness.

He swore next, a string of highly colorful epithets having to do with how much his shoulder hurt. She ignored his complaint and continued pouring orange juice into him, along with a hefty dose of penicillin tablets and the lone dose of morphine in her med kit.

"Enough already with the juice. It tastes like battery acid," he complained.

"You need the liquid and the sugar. You lost a ton of blood."

"Is the bleeding stopped?" he asked.

"Mostly. I got the bullet out and did what cleaning and repair I could, but your shoulder's a mess. You need a good orthopedic surgeon and soon."

He started to shrug, but swore violently at the movement. Finally he gritted out, "Am I going to live?"

"Are you kidding? You're too cussed to die. Even Satan won't have you."

He grinned. "Thanks."

"You're welcome." She took a deep breath. "Ready for the next crisis?"

His expression went deadly and his gaze ranged around the room quickly, as though he was looking for someone to kill. She recoiled from the killer abruptly lying before her.

"What's up?" he bit out.

"We've lost Mia and Emanuel."

He frowned for a moment before his face lit with recollection. "I gave them to Grandma. Told H.O.T. Watch to cover her retreat out the front door."

"What's H.O.T. Watch?"

"The backup you accused me of not having."

She wasn't exactly sure what he meant, but now was not the time for explanations. "We have to find Grandma and the children. The police will be crawling all over Mercado, and once the Colombian Army finds out that Eduardo Lentano and his inner circle are here, they'll come in with guns blazing, too."

He nodded slightly, wincing at even that tiny movement.

She wished she had more painkillers for him, but knowing him he wouldn't have taken them anyway.

"Where's my cell phone?" he asked.

She dug around in the bloody mess that had been his shirt and found the cell phone still in the pocket and covered in blood. "I don't know if it'll work. It's pretty wet."

"You'd be surprised," he muttered as he touched its face.

She listened as he spoke tersely. "I'm shot. Left shoulder's out of commission. Yes, I got emergency field care and am stable. The elderly woman and two children who fled the firefight. I need to know where they went."

Drago listened for a moment and then swore. He muttered to her, "They didn't have time to get telemetry on the building before things went to hell."

Telemetry? What on earth was he talking about? They who?

"Elise. Where would Grandma take the children to hide? She mentioned having a son and daughter in the Army of Freedom. Did she say anything about them living in this area?"

She thought back through her various conversations with the elderly woman. She shook her head regretfully.

Drago was arguing into the phone. "…important assets. I'm not going to leave them behind… No, it's not open to discussion…I'm not leaving until I've got them."

He disconnected the call angrily.

"Were you talking about Mia and Emanuel just now?" she asked.

"Yeah. H.O.T. Watch is going to try to figure out where they've gone. But in a city this size, they could be anywhere. Particularly since Grandma may actually know some of the locals. I don't know how we're going to find the kids, but I swear, Elise. We will."

"Look. They're my responsibility. You need to get to a hospital, and if that means leaving the country, you need to go ahead and do that. I'll stay behind and look for them."

"Not happening," he bit out.

"Why? They're not your job."

"I choose to make them my job."

"But—"

He sat up, swearing, effectively cutting her off as she darted forward to help him.

"But nothing," he ground out. "I couldn't live with myself if I left those kids behind. They were scared out of their minds tonight. I need to know they're safe. That they'll be okay and I didn't scar them for life by getting them kidnapped and hauled into the middle of a shoot-out."

She stared at him in shock.

"What?" he demanded irritably.

"For an arms dealer with no experience around children, you sure do have a soft spot for those kids."

"Are you complaining?" he snapped as he reached for the weapon she'd tossed on the bed when she'd gone to work on him earlier.

"You're not going out in this state. I just got the bleeding stopped and you've only been conscious a few minutes."

"I feel fine."

"You're not fine, and you can barely move without swearing up a blue storm. I've seen plenty of injuries like yours, and you need a couple of months of complete rest to heal."

"Mia and Emanuel don't have a couple of months. They may have only a couple of *hours*."

The panic already bubbling in her gut surged even

harder. "I know that," she replied with desperate calm. "But I'll go look for them. You need to stay here and rest."

He stared at her in disbelief. "Do you seriously think I'm going to let you go out into the war zone this town has just become *alone* to look for those kids?"

"Well, yes."

"Well, *no*," he snarled.

"Why not?" she demanded in utter frustration.

"Because I love you, dammit."

# Chapter 13

Ted didn't know who was more shocked by his declaration, him or her. Elise was staring at him as though she'd just witnessed a miracle.

Shaken to the core of his being, he slung the nylon strap of the gun over his good shoulder. "Stay here. I'll be back when I find them."

"Oh, no you don't! You don't get to say something like that and then just walk out on me."

"Look. Time is against us. We can talk later, but right now we have to find the children."

"I get that, you big lug. But I'm going with you. I doubt you'll make it down to the parking lot by yourself."

"I'll make it," he retorted. But as he took a few steps toward the door, his head felt as if it was floating a foot or two above his body.

"And I'm driving," she declared.

As much as it went against his grain, he couldn't argue

with the logic of that. He let her help him downstairs and to the back of the Jeep. He opened the big duffel bag of gear there and pulled out a black turtleneck sweater. He nearly passed out before Elise managed to slip the thing over his head as gently as she could. She was right. He was in no shape to be running around. But he wasn't kidding. He'd die if he had to in order to find the children and get them and Elise to safety.

Elise lifted his spare Kevlar vest out of the bag of gear. "Please wear this. I'm out of supplies to patch you up with if you get shot again."

He smiled wryly. "I hope that's not the only reason you don't want to see me shot."

"Later," she replied shortly.

He swore under his breath. He might be out of it, but not so much that he'd failed to notice she didn't respond in kind to his declaration of love. What a fool he was.

As she eased the vest up over his arms, it felt as though someone was tearing his arm off. He sucked in air between his clenched teeth as he shrugged the thing into place.

She strapped his utility belt around his waist and hung a pair of earphones around his neck at his direction. He would have preferred using the tiny microphone sewn into his shirt, but Elise had pretty well shredded that when she made a bandage out of his clothing. Not that he was complaining. Being alive was a good thing. Only her quick thinking and trauma-nursing experience had saved him.

He let her help him into the passenger's seat and then she slid behind the wheel. "Where to?" she asked him.

He frowned. "We can't head back to the Army of Freedom headquarters to pick up Grandma's trail. Half the police in Colombia will be there. Is there somewhere we can go to get access to a phone book to look for relatives of hers? Her last name is Ferrosa, right?"

Elise stared ahead, frowning. Then suddenly, her face lit up. "I've got it!"

"Huh?"

"A church. She'll head for a church. It's what she did before. When her house was attacked, she kept talking about how God looks out for His lambs and to have faith in His protection. And she took us to a church the night her village was attacked."

"Makes sense. Any idea where the nearest church is?"

"No. But if we head for a high hill, we should be able to spot it."

She pulled out of the parking lot eagerly.

They'd driven about halfway across Mercado when she turned a corner and slammed on the brakes. Ted groaned aloud as his shoulder screamed in protest. His groan might also have something to do with the police roadblock directly in front of them. It was too late to back up, turn around, and go another way. The police had spotted them, and one was walking forward purposefully toward the Jeep.

"Act drunk," Elise whispered as she threw a blanket at him in the few seconds before the cop gestured for her to roll down the window. He tucked the blanket over his military gear and prayed they didn't get searched. He'd never be able to explain his high-tech military equipment away.

Lolling a little to one side and acting woozy wasn't much of a stretch for him at the moment. Elise asked the policeman irritably, "What's the problem, Officer?"

"We're checking all vehicles for gunmen who might be trying to flee Mercado."

"Only man in this car is my cheating drunk of a husband. Any chance you could shoot him for me?" she snapped. "Three o'clock in the morning and I get a phone call from my girlfriend that she's spotted my husband with some floozy in a bar. And ohmigod, it has to be my friend who's the biggest gossip in Colombia. I'm going to kill him. You might as well arrest me now, Officer—"

The policeman threw up his hands to stop her tirade. Ted tried to act guilty, but it was hard to keep a smile off his face. He settled for slurring, "Come on, baby. I didn't do nuthin' with her. I looove you, dollface."

"Don't you dollface me. I'm divorcing you and taking you for every peso you're worth, you low-life bastard!" She devolved into a furious fit of cussing that would embarrass a sailor.

The policeman interrupted. "There's a curfew in effect. I need you to go directly home and get inside. You understand me?" The man made eye contact with Ted through the window. "Get her home, and you sleep on the couch until she cools off."

Ted nodded fuzzily. "Home. Couch. Got it."

The cop rolled his eyes and waved them through the roadblock. As the flashing lights retreated behind them, Elise let out a loud breath.

"Who'd have guessed a nun knew such foul language?" he commented in amusement.

She flashed him a brief grin as she turned a corner to head uphill.

The road crested a rise, and she stopped the vehicle, asking, "Do you see a bell tower anywhere?"

"Over there." He pointed off to the north.

"Got it." The Jeep rolled forward and she turned to head for the church. Her sense of direction was unerring. Or maybe it was just her mama-bear gene coming to the fore. He estimated they were maybe a half-dozen blocks from the church when another police roadblock came into sight.

"Am I a cheating drunk again?" he asked wryly.

"No, I think we'd better try another tactic. These guys may be in radio contact with the other roadblocks."

Good thinking on her part. But he was at a loss to come up with another tactic. He watched, bemused, as she fished in the pocket of her sweater and came up with her wimple. Aah. Clever.

"Can you take off that gear by yourself?" she asked quickly.

Oh, hell. But it wasn't as if he had any choice. Wincing, he managed to shrug out of the Kevlar vest and utility belt and stow them behind his seat. He awkwardly tossed the blanket over the pile as she tucked the wimple behind her ears.

She glanced over at him and frowned. "That black shirt will have to do. You're a priest. Got it?"

A priest? He blinked, startled. "Uh, okay."

She drove up to the barricade and stopped. "Good evening, Officer. Some trouble afoot tonight?"

"Yes, Sister. There's been a fight at the Devil's Den."

She smiled gently. "I'd appreciate the irony of that if I didn't suspect that people got hurt tonight. All of the police are all right, I hope?"

"Yes, Sister."

"Thank God." She muttered a little something in Latin that Ted didn't recognize, but the policeman crossed himself.

Then the cop asked, "Where are you headed at this hour?"

"Father André—he's just arrived in town—and I are headed over to the church to make sure everything's all right. We heard gunshots."

"There's a curfew."

"I understand. We'll stay at the church for the rest of the night, then. It works out well for us, anyway. Father

André can say matins on time. Perhaps you'll come for the service?"

"Uh, I'm not off duty then," the cop mumbled.

Elise tsked a little. "We haven't seen you for a while at Mass, have we?"

"This Sunday. I promise."

"I'll hold you to that," Elise replied sternly.

The policeman waved them through the roadblock.

"Remind me to take you with me on all my missions where subterfuge is called for," Ted muttered.

"Missions? What kind of missions?" she asked.

He wasn't so out of it that he would spill classified information. He silently reminded himself to watch his tongue. Thankfully, they pulled up in front of a decent-size church and he was saved from having to answer Elise's inconvenient questions.

He followed her gingerly up the front steps, glad she couldn't see him grimace as every step jarred his shoulder. She pushed on one of the tall, carved doors and it swung open slowly. The interior of the church was dimly lit, and a few flickering offering candles burned low on an iron stand just inside the door. Pews that would seat perhaps five hundred people stretched toward the front of the church.

"Hello!" he called out. No answer.

"Hola!" Elise called out in Spanish. "It's me. Sister Elise."

Still no response. His stomach felt like lead. Grandma and the kids *had* to be here. He was at the end of his strength and couldn't go gallivanting across Mercado looking for them. He walked cautiously toward the altar with Elise on his heels. Was there a secret hidey-hole under the altar here, too?

They got to the front and Elise lifted the white linen

table skirt. He pointed his high-intensity flashlight at the stone floor but spotted no seams to indicate there might be a trapdoor. Elise looked close to tears.

"We'll find them," he murmured. "This is a big building. Maybe they're hiding somewhere else."

She nodded and took a wobbly breath, gesturing toward a small door at the back of the nave.

"Let me go first," he told her quietly. He stood to one side of the portal and threw it open, spinning into the space fast. He nearly fainted from the pain that slammed into him and blinked through the whirling darkness. Movement off to his left. He swung his weapon toward it, struggling to focus.

He jerked the weapon up and away from the fast moving object as it barreled into him, shouting, "Drago! I knew you'd come for us!"

Gasping with pain, Ted used his good arm to catch Emanuel as the little boy flung himself against him.

A sob to his right had him swinging toward the new threat, but it was only Elise catching up Mia in a hug against her.

"I knew you would come," Grandma announced from the darkness somewhere on the other side of a large office.

Ted spotted the elderly woman as she emerged from behind the desk, moving slowly. "Are you all right?" he asked her in concern.

"I am not as young as I once was. Running across a big city was a little much for these old bones."

Ted grunted. "I know the feeling."

"We leave now, yes?" she asked.

Elise answered, "There's a curfew. We have to stay here till morning—"

A male voice spoke from behind them and Ted forced his body, through sheer force of will, to turn. He set Emanuel down and pushed the boy behind him, hissing as he used his bad arm to protect the child.

"Not necessary," the man said. "We can go now, if you like."

A man in a black, short-sleeved shirt and white priest's collar was striding down the central aisle toward them.

"And you are?" Ted asked cautiously, his weapon trained, albeit shakily, on the man.

"I am Padre Jorge del Potro. A little bird named Hathaway called me a little while ago. He told me there might be a flock of lambs in need of assistance in my church."

Ted exhaled in relief.

The priest continued, smiling. "The little birdie suggested I call my church superiors. I did so, and they told me these children are under the Holy Roman See's special protection."

Emanuel poked his head out from behind Ted. "God loves little children and watches us specially."

"That he does, child. I am told that in a few minutes, travel documents for all of you will be faxed to me. The Papal Nunciate itself is sending them, apparently. I am told a Father Ambrose in New York City has been very busy the past few days."

Ted glanced over at Elise questioningly, and she smiled back at him. That must be the priest she'd mentioned before. The one who'd sent her here to get Mia and Emanuel. The one he would like to strangle for putting her in such danger…right after he thanked the guy profusely for putting Elise into his path so they could meet.

The fax machine on the desk behind Grandma beeped, and sheets of paper began to spit out of it.

The priest moved across the room to gather up the documents. And that was the last thing Ted saw as his legs gave out from under him and the world went black.

## Chapter 14

Elise lost count of how many times Mia and Emanuel made her swear that Drago was all right on the long flight back to Miami.

The Catholic Church not only took care of the local curfew and permission to pass the roadblocks, but it had a private jet waiting for them when they arrived at the airport in the nearby city of Pasto. The priest had driven the black SUV right up to the plane and he and the pilots had carried Drago, who was still unconscious, aboard.

His shoulder wasn't bleeding and he wasn't showing signs of shock. She suspected he was merely exhausted and overcome by pain and had passed out. She had no idea how he'd even stayed vertical, let alone moving around for so long the way he had been.

"He'll be fine, Emanuel. I swear. He's just sleeping. Superheroes need their rest, too, you know."

"Yes, Mia. His shoulder will be fine. When we get to

America, the finest doctor available will fix it." Although Elise wasn't so sure about that one. She was careful not to make any promises about that.

Grandma and the children finally fell asleep as the night's terror caught up with them. But Elise couldn't do the same. She sat beside Drago where he lay on the floor, holding his hand and praying for him, her lips moving hesitantly through long-forgotten prayers.

Some time later, a faint squeeze of her fingers made her eyes fly open in surprise. Drago was awake. "Oh, thank God," she breathed.

"Am I going to kick the bucket?" he asked wryly.

"You'd better not," she retorted.

"What happened?"

"You passed out. Apparently, even macho men like you have your limits."

He nodded slowly. "I guess we do." His eyes closed for a moment, and when they opened again, infinite sadness swam in them. It was one of the most distressing things she'd ever seen. His emotional withdrawal from her was a tangible thing. It felt as if her heart was being ripped out of her chest as she stared down at him.

"I'm sorry about what I said earlier, Elise. You know. About loving you. I shouldn't have said that."

"I understand. I'd just saved your life and it came out in the heat of the moment. I didn't take it seriously. It's all good—" Her voice broke on the last word and the stream of babbling falling from her mouth stopped.

Oh, God. Her eyes were filling with hot, painful tears. Please, please, please let her not cry. Not in front of him.

"No," he breathed. And then more strongly, "No!"

She looked up from her clenched fists in surprise.

"I was telling the truth, Elise. I do love you. But you never asked for me to chase you all over Colombia like I did. And you darned well didn't ask me to drag you into a firefight with the Army of Freedom and nearly get you and the kids killed."

Shock rendered her nearly speechless. He loved her? She only managed to mumble a shocked, "Oh."

"I was stupid and selfish. I was so focused on my mission that I endangered you and Grandma and the children. I'll never forgive myself for that. I know there's no way to make it up to you. I only hope you'll forgive me someday. If you'll pass me my phone, I'll talk to my boss and make sure the U.S. government does everything in its power to see the children safely settled in America and that they'll never be in danger again."

"And who exactly is your boss?" she sputtered.

He stared up at her blankly for a moment. And then, of all things, he *blushed*. "Uh, Elise. As you may have guessed, I haven't been entirely honest with you."

"You think?" she exclaimed with all the sarcasm she could pack into the words. "I know you're not just some arms dealer. I guessed you might be a soldier or a spy. And after all we've been through, you could tell me your real name, or something close to it."

His gaze slid away from hers, but then returned resolutely. "My name's Theodore Fisher. I'm a captain in the United States Army. I was sent to Colombia to impersonate a dead arms dealer named Drago Cantori. My mission was to find out who he was doing business with and what the customers planned to do with the weapons he was supposed to sell them."

"And the customer was the Army of Freedom?"

He nodded.

"Theodore. Like Alvin and the Chipmunks?"

"I like to think in terms of the dead president, myself,"

he replied dryly. "My friends call me Ted, if you like that better."

She tapped a front tooth with a fingernail. "I don't know. That's an awfully cuddly name for a macho guy like you. It'll take some getting used to."

He stopped in the act of saying whatever he'd been about to say and stared. "Does that mean…" He trailed off.

She waited him out while he caught up with the conversation. Sometimes men could be so slow on the uptake. Although in his defense, he was badly injured.

"…does that mean you don't hate me?" he asked tentatively.

"I don't hate you," she confirmed.

"And does that mean you might actually like me a little bit?"

"It does. And I do."

"Like me?"

"No, you big, sweet idiot. I love you."

He sat up fast and she reached for him reflexively as he sucked in a hard breath. In spite of his obvious pain, he reached for her with both arms and drew her close in the big, warm hug she would never tire of. She laid her head carefully on his good shoulder.

"How much do you love me?" he asked cautiously.

"Why?" she replied with equal caution. "What did you have in mind?"

He paused a long time and then asked soberly, "Has Father Ambrose already found a family to adopt Mia and Emanuel?"

"Not to my knowledge. He usually spends a few months helping refugee children acclimate to American culture and learn a little English first. He likes to get to know the children so he can place them in a home that will be ideal for the kids based on their needs."

"What do you suppose the odds are that he'd consider us to adopt them?"

She leaned back to stare at him in confusion. She said blankly, "But we're not even married."

He grinned down at her. "That's easy enough to fix."

"Excuse me?"

"You are planning to marry me, aren't you?"

"Well, yes. But I figured I'd have to spend a while longer convincing you that you can't live without me."

He laughed and winced simultaneously. "I'm already there. Thing is, can you live without me?"

"Not a chance."

"So you'll marry me? Even if we don't get the kids?"

"Absolutely…Ted." His real name felt strange on her tongue. "Yeah. That's weird. I may have to keep calling you Drago—"

But then he was kissing her and she didn't care what his name was. Cheering erupted from somewhere behind them and Mia and Emanuel jumped on top of her and Ted. They opened their arms to include the children in the embrace and Ted manfully swallowed his pain. If possible, she loved him even a little more in that moment. She'd never met as generous a man in all her life.

She glanced up and met Grandma's smiling gaze. "I suppose now's as good a time as any to tell you I'm not really a nun."

"I've known that all along, child."

"But how?" Elise stuttered.

Grandma laughed gaily. "Father Ambrose told me that day when you called him."

"But you said—"

"And I meant it. Any woman who would risk her life to

save two children she's never met deserves to be a saint. And any woman who would risk her life for a man, like you have for this one, deserves a long and happy life with him."

Elise laughed and looked over at her man. "From your lips to God's ear, Grandma."

# Chapter 15

Father Ambrose was as fussy as ever, ushering Elise and Ted into his office and making a production out of preparing tea for them. She sat down, savoring the feel of his hand resting lightly on her shoulder. She'd never get enough of him.

The priest asked, "Are you ready for the big day?"

Ted smiled down at her and she answered for both of them. "Definitely. I'm just sorry my parents aren't here to share it."

"Aah, child, but they are. They're always watching over you from heaven."

She smiled and took a sip of her tea as Ted asked, "Any news on Grandma's green card?"

"Why, yes. Her residency documents came through a few days ago. She's agreed to stay with Mia and Emanuel indefinitely. Sadly, her surviving son and daughter died when the last remnants of the Army of Freedom were destroyed in Mercado last month. With her home gone, she has nothing to go back to Colombia for. She will provide some much needed stability in Mia and Emanuel's lives."

Elise nodded. "I think maybe she needs the kids as much as they need her."

The priest nodded solemnly. Then he asked Ted, "How's your shoulder doing?"

"Better. I can't be in the Special Forces anymore, but I have almost full use of it now."

"Have you decided what you're going to do next, my son?"

Elise smiled proudly as Ted answered, "I've been thinking about medical school. After all those years I spent killing people, I think I'd like to spend a while healing people."

After a moment of reflective silence, Father Ambrose commented to her, "So what did you think of being a nun?"

She laughed ruefully. "I think I'm not cut out for a life of such hard-core self-denial. You're made of sterner stuff than I, Padre."

He laughed gaily. "It was more difficult for you without the calling we people of the cloth answer to. I expect your wedding gown will look much better on you than a wimple."

"Thank you." Her heart filled with peace at his words. A wedding. Her wedding. Hers and Ted's. "It's almost time, Father."

"Impatient to become Elise Fisher, are you?" He made a small production of having them each sign their marriage license. As she rose with the intent to go change into her white lace gown, Father Ambrose raised his hand to stop her.

"Before we go and marry you two off, I have a small wedding present for the two you."

"You didn't have to," she and Ted exclaimed in the perfect unison they seemed to do so many things these days.

"Aah, but I did." He passed them a plain manila envelope with a broad smile. "I need both of you to sign these."

She pulled out a thick sheaf of legal papers and gasped as she spied the title: *Petition for Adoption in the State of New York.* Ted swept her in his arms and squeezed her so tightly and so long she thought she might pass out.

Finally he whispered, "Our very own family. Now I have everything I ever dreamed of."

His shirt front absorbed her welling tears as Father Ambrose continued, "You and Ted were willing to give your lives for Mia and Emanuel, and the children adore you both. Who am I to break apart a family that God has clearly brought together?"

Elise fanned herself vigorously with the papers, unable to stop herself from babbling in her joy. "I'm going to cry and then my mascara will run and I'll look like a clown and Mia was so hoping I'd look like a princess today."

Ted passed her a handkerchief and waited while she dabbed at her eyes and collected herself. Then he murmured down to her, "Let's go make our family official, shall we?"

As she stepped out into the church to the strains of wedding music, Elise reflected on what a funny thing faith was. It was a lot like love. Just when she thought she'd lost them both, they went and found her again.

Thanks to a man with a giant heart, a pair of orphans

a lot like her, and a wily old priest who knew her better than she knew herself. Maybe redemption was possible in this world, after all, with a little faith and a lot of love.

\* \* \* \* \*

# SUSPENSE

Heartstopping stories of intrigue and mystery—
where true love always triumphs.

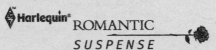

## COMING NEXT MONTH
### AVAILABLE JANUARY 31, 2012

# REQUEST YOUR FREE BOOKS!
## 2 FREE NOVELS PLUS 2 FREE GIFTS!

 Harlequin®

## ROMANTIC
## *SUSPENSE*
### *Sparked by Danger, Fueled by Passion.*

---

**YES!** Please send me 2 FREE Harlequin® Romantic Suspense novels and my 2 FREE gifts (gifts are worth about $10). After receiving them, if I don't wish to receive any more books, I can return the shipping statement marked "cancel." If I don't cancel, I will receive 4 brand-new novels every month and be billed just $4.49 per book in the U.S. or $5.24 per book in Canada. That's a saving of at least 14% off the cover price! It's quite a bargain! Shipping and handling is just 50¢ per book in the U.S. and 75¢ per book in Canada.* I understand that accepting the 2 free books and gifts places me under no obligation to buy anything. I can always return a shipment and cancel at any time. Even if I never buy another book, the two free books and gifts are mine to keep forever.

240/340 HDN FEFR

Name _____
　　　　　　　　　　　　(PLEASE PRINT)

Address _____ Apt. # _____

City _____ State/Prov. _____ Zip/Postal Code _____

Signature (if under 18, a parent or guardian must sign) _____

### Mail to the **Reader Service:**
**IN U.S.A.:** P.O. Box 1867, Buffalo, NY 14240-1867
**IN CANADA:** P.O. Box 609, Fort Erie, Ontario L2A 5X3

Not valid for current subscribers to Harlequin Romantic Suspense books.

**Want to try two free books from another line?**
**Call 1-800-873-8635 or visit www.ReaderService.com.**

* Terms and prices subject to change without notice. Prices do not include applicable taxes. Sales tax applicable in N.Y. Canadian residents will be charged applicable taxes. Offer not valid in Quebec. This offer is limited to one order per household. All orders subject to credit approval. Credit or debit balances in a customer's account(s) may be offset by any other outstanding balance owed by or to the customer. Please allow 4 to 6 weeks for delivery. Offer available while quantities last.

**Your Privacy**—The Reader Service is committed to protecting your privacy. Our Privacy Policy is available online at www.ReaderService.com or upon request from the Reader Service.

We make a portion of our mailing list available to reputable third parties that offer products we believe may interest you. If you prefer that we not exchange your name with third parties, or if you wish to clarify or modify your communication preferences, please visit us at www.ReaderService.com/consumerschoice or write to us at Reader Service Preference Service, P.O. Box 9062, Buffalo, NY 14269. Include your complete name and address.

HRS11B

Discover a touching new trilogy from
*USA TODAY* bestselling author

# Janice Kay Johnson

## Between Love and Duty

As the eldest brother of three, Duncan MacLachlan
is used to being in control and maintaining an
emotional distance; as a police captain it's his job.
But when he meets Jane Brooks, Duncan soon finds
his control slipping away. Together, they fight for a
young boy's future, and soon Duncan finds himself
hoping to build a future with Jane.

*Available February 2012*

## From Father to Son
*(March 2012)*

## The Call of Bravery
*(April 2012)*

*Louisa Morgan loves being around children.
So when she has the opportunity to tutor bedridden Ellie,
she's determined to bring joy back into the motherless
girl's world. Can she also help Ellie's father open his
heart again? Read on for a sneak peek of*

## THE COWBOY FATHER

*by Linda Ford,
available February 2012 from Love Inspired Historical.*

Why had Louisa thought she could do this job? A bubble of self-pity whispered she was totally useless, but Louisa ignored it. She wasn't useless. She could help Ellie if the child allowed it.

Emmet walked her out, waiting until they were out of earshot to speak. "I sense you and Ellie are not getting along."

"Ellie has lost her freedom. On top of that, everything is new. Familiar things are gone. Her only defense is to exert what little independence she has left. I believe she will soon tire of it and find there are more enjoyable ways to pass the time."

He looked doubtful. Louisa feared he would tell her not to return. But after several seconds' consideration, he sighed heavily. "You're right about one thing. She's lost everything. She can hardly be blamed for feeling out of sorts."

"She hasn't lost everything, though." Her words were quiet, coming from a place full of certainty that Emmet was more than enough for this child. "She has you."

"She'll always have me. As long as I live." He clenched his fists. "And I fully intend to raise her in such a way that even if something happened to me, she would never feel like I was gone. I'd be in her thoughts and in her actions every day."

Peace filled Louisa. "Exactly what my father did."

Their gazes connected, forged a single thought about fathers and daughters...how each needed the other. How sweet the relationship was.

Louisa tipped her head away first. "I'll see you tomorrow."

Emmet nodded. "Until tomorrow then."

She climbed behind the wheel of their automobile and turned toward home. She admired Emmet's devotion to his child. It reminded her of the love her own father had lavished on Louisa and her sisters. Louisa smiled as fond memories of her father filled her thoughts. Ellie was a fortunate child to know such love.

*Louisa understands what both father and daughter are going through. Will her compassion help them heal—and form a new family? Find out in*
*THE COWBOY FATHER*
*by Linda Ford, available February 14, 2012.*

**Love Inspired Books celebrates 15 years of inspirational romance in 2012! February puts the spotlight on Love Inspired Historical, with each book celebrating family and the special place it has in our hearts. Be sure to pick up all four Love Inspired Historical stories, available February 14, wherever books are sold.**

USA TODAY **bestselling author**

# Sarah Morgan

**brings readers another enchanting story**

# ONCE A FERRARA WIFE...

When Laurel Ferrara is summoned back to Sicily
by her estranged husband, billionaire
Cristiano Ferrara, Laurel knows things are about
to heat up. And Cristiano's power is a potent
reminder of his Sicilian dynasty's unbreakable rule:
once a Ferrara wife, always a Ferrara wife....

**Sparks fly this February**